3 2410 01837 8391

Into the Wild

Into the Wild

a novel by
Sarah Beth Durst

razOr
bill

Into the Wild

RAZORBILL

Published by the Penguin Group
Penguin Young Readers Group
345 Hudson Street, New York, New York 10014, U.S.A.
Penguin Group (USA) Inc., 375 Hudson Street, New York, New York 10014, U.S.A.
Penguin Group (Canada), 90 Eglinton Avenue East, Suite 700, Toronto, Ontario, Canada
M4P 2Y3 (a division of Pearson Penguin Canada Inc.)
Penguin Books Ltd, 80 Strand, London WC2R 0RL, England
Penguin Ireland, 25 St Stephen's Green, Dublin 2, Ireland (a division of Penguin Books
Ltd)
Penguin Group (Australia), 250 Camberwell Road, Camberwell, Victoria 3124, Australia
(a division of Pearson Australia Group Pty Ltd)
Penguin Books India Pvt Ltd, 11 Community Centre, Panchsheel Park, New Delhi – 110
017, India
Penguin Group (NZ), Cnr Airborne and Rosedale Roads, Albany, Auckland 1310, New
Zealand (a division of Pearson New Zealand Ltd)
Penguin Books (South Africa) (Pty) Ltd, 24 Sturdee Avenue, Rosebank, Johannesburg
2196, South Africa

Penguin Books Ltd, Registered Offices: 80 Strand, London WC2R 0RL, England

10 9 8 7 6 5 4 3 2

Library of Congress Cataloging-in-Publication Data is available

Printed in the United States of America

For my mother and my daughter

You are holding in your hands my wish in the wishing well. Thank you to everyone who made my dream come true: Andrea Somberg (my agent/hero), Ben Schrank, Jessica Rothenberg, Andy Ball, Liesa Abrams, Tamora Pierce, my family and friends, and all the other fantastic people who helped make this book a reality. And most of all, thank you to my husband/prince Adam. You are my magic. This book is as much yours as it is mine.

Part One

The Woods

Chapter One
The Monster Under the Bed

In the darkness, the heart of the fairy tale waited . . .

Julie picked up a scrap of shoelace. Once upon a time, it had been an entire sneaker. "Look what you did," she said, wiggling it under her bed.

Snapping out a green vine, the Wild snatched the lace.

"Hey!" She dropped to her knees and peered under the bed. It's not fair, she grumbled to herself. Worst most people had under their beds was dust bunnies. The Wild, a tangled mass of green, tried to tuck itself back into the shadows under her bed, but one vine—the newest—couldn't fit. "Oh, great," Julie said. "Not again." She flattened onto her stomach to see it better. The new growth was pale green with tuliplike leaves that cradled a half-laced, tan-colored boot—the fate of her poor sneaker.

The Wild had swallowed and transformed it.

Note to self, Julie thought, throwing things at the Wild was not the brightest move. In her defense, though, when she threw the shoe, it was 2 a.m. and the vines were snoring. "Mom!" she called, getting up. "It happened again!"

"Be there in a minute!" her mom called back.

This was her third pair this month. Julie scrounged through her closet. She was pretty sure that all she had now were left shoes. And a pair of flip-flops—bright sunflower yellow flip-flops. Perfect footwear for October in Massachusetts. She put them on and grimaced. Her naked toes looked like plump breakfast sausages. Maybe no one will notice, she thought hopefully.

Mom came into the room with a kitchen knife. Her eyes swept expertly over the room and settled on Julie's feet. So much for no one noticing. Julie wiggled her toes.

"I'm sorry," Mom said. "I could try putting it back in the basement." Leaves rustled as the Wild pressed itself farther under the bed. The vine with the boot quivered and began to slide back into the green. "Quick, catch it!"

Julie scrambled forward and grabbed the boot. The vines squirmed. She leaned back, pulling against the vines with her full weight. "Why do we always have to guard it?" she complained. "Can't one of your friends take a turn?" She shot a look at Mom. Julie hadn't meant to ask that. The words had slipped out before she'd thought about them.

"Julie, watch the vine."

4

She turned back as the Wild struggled, leaves flapping against the underside of the mattress. Julie stepped on the new vine with her flip-flopped foot, holding it steady. Businesslike, Mom sawed off the boot. Green ooze stained the carpet and spattered Julie's toes.

Mom eyed the boot critically. "Unfinished Seven League Boot. I'd say it's about a three-mile boot." She tucked the boot under her arm, then fetched her special key from her bedroom and unlocked the linen closet. Rubbing the excess ooze off her foot, Julie trailed after her.

She peeked over Mom's shoulder into the closet. All the shelves were stuffed with the Wild's creations: cloaks, purses, wands, hats, picnic baskets. The Wild had made a *lot* of items. It desperately wanted to grow again.

She looked again at Mom. Was she just going to ignore the question? "You didn't answer me," Julie said.

"Oh, pumpkin, not now, please," Mom said. "We could put it back in the basement. But that's the best we can do."

Ugh, that wasn't a solution. Last time they had kept it in the basement, it had pried all the plumbing out of the walls and transformed half of the hot water heater. Julie had had to take cold showers for two weeks after that. "Never mind," Julie said. The Wild was calmest under Julie's bed, and it was weak enough that Mom was willing to allow it to stay there. Maybe the Wild thought Julie would help it grow. Fat chance of that.

Mom locked the closet door and handed Julie her special works-on-any-door key. She kissed Julie on the forehead. "Don't be blue. It's only a shoe." And then she smiled. "How's that for a rhyme?"

"Very rhyme-y," Julie said.

As her mother went downstairs, Julie locked her bedroom door with the special key and then returned the key to her mother's jewelry box. Mom *never* answered her straight-out. Why did they have to have this permanent houseguest? Why couldn't she just once have a normal morning without lost shoes or locked doors or any of it? As she trudged down to the kitchen, she tried to imagine what a normal morning would be like. She pictured her mother wearing an apron and a '50s-mom smile and handing Julie a paper bag lunch. And of course, Julie's father would be there, sitting at the kitchen table and reading the newspaper. He'd put it down when Julie came into the kitchen, and he'd say . . .

Her mother handed her a Cheerios box. "Did you lock the door?"

For a second, Julie blinked at her. She had almost pictured him there, maybe in a bathrobe and slippers or in a suit and tie, ready for work, whatever that would be. He'd have an office job, be home in time for dinner, and he'd complain about the commute, like other dads . . . She could almost see his face, smiling at her . . .

"Did you hear me?" Mom asked. "Did you lock the door?"

Julie sighed as the daydream vanished. "Mom, please."

"Julie, it's important."

"Yeah, I know," she said. "I'm not a baby."

Her mom cooed. "My wittle baby-waby." She sounded so exactly like a cartoon mouse that Julie laughed in spite of herself. Her mom made a fish face. "Oobe snooby uppy wuppy."

Julie made a fish face back at her. "Uppy snuppy wuppy puppy."

Her mom smiled, and Julie grinned back. And for an instant, everything was okay. Julie started on her cereal as her mom fixed her age makeup in the reflection in the microwave door. She wore just enough to look the appropriate age for a mother of a twelve-year-old. Julie watched as her mom wet the tip of a brown eyeliner and darkened a wrinkle on her forehead. Skillfully, she blended in the new shadow. With makeup, she almost looked ordinary, Julie thought. Of course, all the makeup in the world couldn't hide her mother's most recognizable feature: she had amazing hair, the color of wheat and the texture of silk, which she kept bobbed short, up above her ears.

Julie wondered what her father would have thought of Mom's short hair. Suddenly, her cereal was hard to swallow. Why was she thinking about him so much this morning?

She should be worrying about how to blend in at school despite her bright yellow flip-flops. Of course, if no one guessed who her mother was from the hair, then no one would guess their family secret from Julie's feet. It wasn't like her footwear was the biggest tip-off around.

Finishing the age makeup, her mother lifted the cloth over the kitchen mirror. "Well?" she asked.

"*Eh, you look terrible,*" the mirror said. "*How many times have I told you that pink is not your color, and what are those? Slacks? You're wearing slacks?*" Her mom dropped the cloth back down.

Compared to a talking mirror, what was a pair of sandals? Today was going to be fine. Or at least it would be if she wasn't late. Glancing at the clock, Julie said, "Gotta go." Grabbing her jacket and backpack, she headed for the door.

"Wait a minute, young lady."

Julie stopped, hand on the door. "What?" she said. Her mother pecked her on the forehead. "Have an uneventful day," Mom said.

With a backward wave, Julie sprinted out the door. Down the driveway, she saw the yellow of the school bus through the red and gold maple leaves. She was going to miss it! Backpack bouncing on her shoulders, she ran for it. Her shoes slapped her feet. The school bus turned from West Street onto Crawford Street. The brakes squeaked as it stopped.

Up ahead, she saw Gillian—book bag in one hand, trumpet case in the other—hopping from foot to foot. "You're almost late," she said as Julie skidded to a stop in front of the bus door. She didn't have to say it: friends don't let friends sit alone on the school bus.

"Happened again," Julie managed to pant.

They slid into a seat as the bus lurched forward. "What was it this time?" Gillian asked as she balanced her trumpet case on her lap.

Julie peeked around the bus seat to make sure no one was listening. "Boot," she whispered. "Supposed to let you go three miles with one step."

Gillian whistled. "Wow," she said. "You could ace gym with that."

Julie shushed her. "I *told* you—"

"I know. Super-secret. Sorry," Gillian said. She too looked to see if anyone was listening, and then she settled back down in her seat. "But don't you think it's cool?"

"Not exactly the word I was thinking of," Julie said, looking down at her exposed toes, and Gillian giggled. Julie grinned back. At least there was one person in this school who knew Julie's weirdness wasn't her fault. Gillian was even loyal enough to think it was cool, once she'd gotten used to the idea. She'd known about it for two years now—ever since she'd walked in on Julie's brother talking to a mirror (and the mirror talking back). That mirror never did shut up. Neither did Julie's brother.

For the rest of the bus ride, they talked about other things: the Halloween dance, Gillian's band tryouts, Julie's history quiz. Gillian left her at the school entrance. "Luck on the Wallace quiz."

"Luck at band," Julie said.

Gillian held out her pinky, and Julie shook it with her pinky. Julie wished (not for the first time) that her locker was next to Gillian's. So not fair. Mom could have chosen any last name she wanted after she escaped the Wild Wood—and yet Julie Marchen was stuck with a locker near the likes of Kristen March.

There was no way Kristen wasn't going to notice the flip-flops. If the school had had fashion police, Kristen would have been their captain. Leaving Gillian, Julie slunk toward her locker. Why should she care if Kristen noticed? I don't care, she told herself. No one was going to be able to guess their secret from a single pair of shoes.

Switching her homework books with her books for the first three periods, she risked a glance across the hall. Kristen tossed her hair—her infamous reversible part. Even with a mother who owned a hair salon, Julie couldn't get her frizz to do that flip. I don't care, she repeated, but she eavesdropped anyway.

"I was going to be a princess," Kristen said to her gaggle

of friends. "I had a tiara and the whole bit." Of course she was, Julie thought. She didn't have to worry about accidentally completing a fairy-tale event.

Her flock said, "Ooh."

"It's all Dad's fault," Kristen said. "He's *impossible*. Of all the weekends to want to go to Vermont, he picks this one. It's so *unfair*."

Julie sucked in a breath. Any other day Kristen's words might not have hit her so hard, but today . . . She felt as if she'd been punched in the gut. *Unfair?* Spending a weekend with a dad was unfair? Kristen had no idea what *unfair* meant.

Turning her back on Kristen, Julie faced her locker. She was okay with Kristen being beautiful and thin and having tons of friends who worshiped her, but Julie would have given anything to have a dad to spend a weekend with. Or even to know what he looked like. She smoothed the collage of illustrations on the inside of her locker door. *Rapunzel, Rapunzel, let down your hair*, each prince said. She didn't even know if he looked like any of them.

She closed the locker with a sigh—loud enough, apparently, to be heard across the hall, because she heard giggling from Kristen's friends. "Isn't it a little late for the beach?" Kristen called. Her voice seemed super-loud, and Julie felt dozens of eyes looking at her and her feet. "Or are you just early for the Halloween dance?" Kristen's flock of friends burst into peals of laughter, and Julie hunched her shoulders as if she could plug her ears with them.

Too bad she couldn't crawl under a rock and hibernate until middle school passed. Would anyone really mind if she opted out of the whole junior high experience? Mom hadn't had to go through it. Maybe, Julie thought as she trudged to class, I can find a nice, doorless tower.

Chapter Two
The Hair Salon

Goldie plopped down in the hairdresser chair. "Look at me!" she wailed. "Oh, just look at me!" Zel peered at her friend's flawless baby-doll face and crown of golden ringlets and said a silent prayer for patience. Once a month, Goldie was in Zel's salon moaning as if she'd suddenly turned green and bald, when in truth, she was the picture of perfection. But it was no use telling her that. And it was no use telling her to make an appointment first. Goldie waved an issue of *Glamour* in the air in front of Zel. "I'm unfashionable!"

Before Zel could respond, she heard a sheep baa outside. She winced: her 10:30 was here early, and she hadn't come alone. "Excuse me," she said to both Goldie and her other customer, Linda. She hurried around the reception desk to the door. "Mary, please, leave it outside. Board of Health regulations."

"I'm trying, Zel," Mary called as she wrestled to tie the sheep's leash to a bike rack. The lamb fought her as if it were rabid. Mary thwapped its head. "Behave."

The lamb bit her.

Zel felt a headache forming, but she tried to be sympathetic. After all, she wasn't the one with the obsessed sheep. "Fine. Bring it in. But it has to stay in the manicure room." The lamb baa-ed triumphantly, and Zel gave it her best steely look. "But no poop on the floor. You use the toilet or you don't go at all."

"Baa?"

"And flush this time," Zel said.

Meekly, the lamb followed Mary inside.

Pausing at the reception desk, Zel marked Mary Hadda in her appointment book and scanned the rest of her schedule. She had a double load today with Gretel out. (Gretel had broken her new sugar-free diet again, and it had disagreed with her.) Zel glanced at the clock: 10:05. So far, the salon had three customers: Goldie, Mary, and one of the town librarians, Linda. Not to mention the lamb.

Zel was already behind, and today was the day she'd persuaded her mother to leave the Wishing Well Motel in the hands (or paws, actually) of one of the guests and come for a haircut. The extra appointment would make Zel even later.

Maybe she should take Gretel's suggestion and ask Julie to help out after school.

At the thought of her daughter, Zel swallowed a sudden lump in her throat. Her baby girl. Lately, it felt like shouting across the Grand Canyon to even try to talk to her. At least she had made her laugh this morning. That was rare these days.

Zel sighed. Sometimes she understood why her own adoptive mother had locked her in a tower. It was hard to watch the person she loved more than her own life grow distant. Each time her daughter rolled her eyes at her, Zel felt her heart twist. She didn't want to wait nine or ten years for Julie to like her again.

The lamb baa-ed vigorously as Mary dragged it into the manicure room, and Zel winced. She really should insist Julie come work. She could use the help, plus it would mean extra mother-daughter time—and, Zel thought wryly, I won't have to find a spare tower in the suburbs.

Closing the appointment book, Zel went to finish trimming Linda's hair. "Did I hear a sheep out there?" Linda asked.

"Sick dog," Zel said. "Now, bend your head down." Linda obeyed and Zel ran her fingers through the back of her hair to check for evenness. All she needed to do was think of a way to make Julie come without Julie immediately assuming her mother was trying to ruin her life. Not an easy task. "You have any books on handling teenage daughters?" she asked lightly.

"Dozens," Linda said. "Self-help books fly off the shelves these days, but that's not what people need." She waved her arm for emphasis, and Zel hopped out of the way. "What people *really* need are more good, old-fashioned stories. A dozen stories can teach people more about how to live their lives than a hundred Ph.D. studies."

"Uh-huh," Zel said. She knew stories—firsthand—and even though she could joke about it, a tower wasn't going to help her with Julie any more than the perfect porridge was going to make Goldie like herself more.

"We've lost our roots, lost ourselves in fads," Linda said. "I tell you, a fresh influx of stories could solve most of the world's problems."

The problem with being a hairdresser, Zel thought, was that you had to listen politely to everyone's pet theories, right or wrong. She was tempted to tell her how Gretel had battled bulimia, how Snow White's marriage had crumbled (her prince hadn't wanted a wife with a personality), how Sleeping Beauty . . . No, stories hadn't helped Zel's friends, but Zel let Linda prattle on.

Moving to the waiting chairs, Goldie paraded her magazines in front of Mary. "What do you think of that one?" she said. "Or, ooh, how about this one?"

Mary's own hair was dyed purple. "I like that one."

"That's a *man*."

"Oops, my bad," Mary said. Goldie grumbled to herself as Mary eyed her critically. "But seriously, Goldie, have you thought about trying bald?"

Goldie was still shrieking when Rapunzel's adoptive mother, Dame Gothel Marchen, walked in. "Oh, my," Gothel said mildly. "One of those days, is it?"

Goldie blanched, instantly silent, and Zel grinned. Her mom had that effect on people. In a purple sweat suit, Gothel looked like someone's sweet grandma, fresh from the Northcourt Pool Shuffleboard League. She had a face as wrinkled as a walnut and hair as frizzed as a gone-to-seed dandelion. She looked like an innocent elderly lady—and, in point of fact, she hadn't boiled a child in years. But when she smiled at Goldilocks and said, "Goldie, dear, you look lovely. Now, why don't you run along home?"—Goldie bolted out the door.

Zel was torn between wanting to laugh and wanting to smack her head against the wall. "Mother, please! You can't do that to customers!" Behind Gothel, Zel saw Mary inch across the chairs toward the doors—preparing to flee. No customers was *not* better than too many customers. "*Mother.*"

Without glancing at Mary, Gothel said, "No, you stay, dear. You need it." Mary froze. From the manicure room, the lamb baa-ed and kicked frantically at the door. "Sheep?" Gothel asked.

"Sick dog," Linda said.

"Would you like me to take a look?" Gothel offered.

Instant silence from the manicure room.

Gothel's cheek twitched, and for a second, Zel thought she saw . . . No, her mother couldn't be bothered by people fearing her. "Pity," Gothel murmured. "It would have made a lovely shish kebob."

Mary paled.

"She's kidding," Zel said.

"Of course I am." Gothel smiled sweetly. "I wouldn't hurt a lamb."

Zel rolled her eyes. She had clearly imagined that flicker of emotion—her mother enjoyed feeding her reputation. "Oh, Mother." Shaking her head, Zel put down her shears and went to hug her. It was time for her mother to quit the wicked witch routine. She didn't even use her powers anymore. Of course, there were a few frogs around Gothel's motel that Zel had her suspicions about, but everyone needed a hobby. So long as it didn't cause the Wild to grow too fast, she wasn't going to ask. She guided her mother to the shampoo chair and fastened the nylon smock around her neck. "You'd have better social skills if you got out more," Zel said. "You spend too much time at that motel."

"Are you nagging me, Rapunzel?" Gothel asked with an edge to her voice.

"Yes," Zel said sternly.

Gothel cackled. Mary flinched at the sound, but Zel couldn't help smiling. She loved her mother's laugh. In the years since they'd escaped the Wild, Gothel's laugh had changed from overtly evil to delicious and free.

In the shampoo chair, Gothel leaned backward. Running warm water, Zel wet her hair. "So what am I missing that's so special?" Gothel asked.

"Well, I don't know." A single mother with her own business to run, Zel wasn't an expert on Northboro's social scene. She added shampoo to Gothel's hair and worked it into a lather. "But you should get out more. Not just for haircuts." She shouldn't be so tied to her responsibilities all the time. She was sacrificing her freedom in her efforts to protect her freedom.

"Saw Ruby doing stand-up at the Dew Drop Inn on Friday night," Mary offered tentatively. "She did her Princess Who Never Laughed routine. And Saturday's karaoke. Harp can hold a tune, if you don't mind six renditions of 'Giants in the Sky.'"

Gothel humphed as Zel rinsed.

"We'll continue this in one second," Zel said. "I have to put Linda under the dryer." She led Linda to a dryer and switched on the heat. "Just a couple of minutes," she told Linda, "and then I'll even out the ends."

She returned to Gothel and towel-dried her hair. "I mean it. You work too hard." She brought her mother to one of the cutting chairs. "You never take a night off." Separating clumps of hair, she flattened one between her fingers and clipped the ends.

Gothel smiled affectionately at Zel's reflection in the salon mirror. "You're a sweet girl, you know that?"

Zel smiled back. Years ago, they weren't so close. Of course, years ago, Gothel had her locked in a tower, but regardless . . . If Zel and Gothel could become close, there was hope for Zel and Julie, wasn't there? Maybe Gothel could talk to Julie. Maybe she could convince Julie to come work at the salon after school.

Zel realized she had the perfect solution to both her problems. "Why don't you come to dinner with Julie and me tonight? We're having Snow's seven, so adding another plate's not a problem."

Gothel sighed and said, "It's not a good time. Dances and midterms and so forth. Kids start sneaking in wanting to make wishes." In a nasal voice, she imitated, "'I wish for Bobby Who-si-whats-it to ask me to the dance.' 'I wish for Susie Q to notice me.'"

Zel glanced at Linda. The blow dryer was on, and chances were good the librarian couldn't hear her. It's fine that Mother's talking freely, Zel thought. She made a mental note that sometime she should check how loud the dryer really was.

"As soon as the sun sets, I have to keep the well under

constant watch. Even barbed wire doesn't keep the little toads out." Gothel sighed again, and for a moment, she looked her age—all the many centuries. Zel's heart ached for her. She had to be able to give her mother one night of rest.

"Can't someone else watch for you?" Zel asked. There were plenty of their kind in Northboro who understood how important it was to keep the well inactive. One of them could guard it for an evening.

Gothel shook her head. "I don't need a night out."

Zel flicked Gothel's shoulder with her finger. "Don't move your head. Yes, you do. You look tired." It was too bad, Zel thought, that the well had proved indestructible. Dismantling it would have saved her mother a lot of worry.

The mirror in front of them said, *"Oh, I have to agree. Those bags under your eyes . . . Not the fairest, most definitely not."*

Zel shot another look at Linda. To her relief, Linda didn't seem alarmed by the talking mirror. Surely the dryer was too loud for her to hear. Linda patted her bangs. "Another minute," Zel shouted to her.

"I can't do it," Gothel said firmly.

Zel played her trump card: "Julie would be thrilled to see you."

Gothel hesitated, and Zel began to hope. "Ursa has

been doing some maid work at the motel recently," Gothel said slowly. "She's very good at making beds, and she has a knack for noticing things out of place. I suppose I could ask her."

"Her husband and son could watch with her," Zel persisted. "No one will mess with the three of them." Julie would be so pleased to have her grandmother come to dinner. It would help make up for Snow's seven being there.

Gothel chuckled. "You always get what you want, don't you?"

With a sharp and sudden pain, Zel thought of her husband, lost so long ago. For an instant, she couldn't breathe. She smiled weakly. "Nearly always."

Chapter Three
After School

Waiting for the bus with Gillian at the end of the school day, Julie saw the orange Subaru speed into the school parking lot. "Oh, no," she said. Hadn't her day been bad enough? She wished she could melt into the sidewalk.

Gillian saw it too. "Maybe the bus will get here first?"

No such luck. Julie watched the car swing into two parking spaces. "Don't get out of the car. Don't get out of the car," Julie said under her breath. But her mom's friend Cindy got out of her orange car and waved cheerily at Julie.

"At least you don't have to take the bus," Gillian said.

"You want a ride?" Julie said.

"Uh, no, thanks."

Bangle bracelets sparkled on her arm as Cindy waved. "It's like a car accident," Kristen March said loudly, behind Julie. "You don't want to look, but you can't help it." Cindy's chosen outfit of the day was a yellow taffeta top, pink Lycra pants, and clear plastic '80s jelly shoes. "Yoo-hoo, Joo-lie!" Cindy called. "Over here!"

All the kids on the sidewalk turned to look at Julie. Behind her, she heard Kristen sputter in laugher. "Joo-lie," Kristen cooed, "I think she stole your Halloween costume." Knowing her face was flushed tomato red, Julie speed-walked across the parking lot. She felt dozens of eyes boring into her back.

"Darling, how are you?" Cindy said. "How was your day? Ooh, I think that boy is looking at you!" She pointed at a sandy-haired eighth grader.

Julie slunk into the car. "Please. Just drive."

"All-righty-roo!" Cindy jumped into the driver's seat, threw the stick into reverse, and flew back out of the parking spaces. She squealed the brakes. "Sorry!" Cindy called out the window.

Julie looked over her shoulder at Gillian and mouthed, "Help me."

Gillian held her hand to her ear like a phone and mouthed back, "Call me."

Switching on the radio, Cindy bopped to an old Britney Spears song as she peeled out of the parking lot. Soon, the school was out of sight behind them—Julie wished it was out of sight, out of mind. She leaned her head against the window and watched the Northboro landmarks zoom by:

the Dairy Hut, Agway's ten-foot rooster, Bigelow Nurseries. Ever since Kristen had mentioned her weekend with her dad, Julie hadn't been able to stop thinking about her own father. In English, she'd been singled out twice for not paying attention. In math, she'd messed up problems. In history . . . The history quiz had included the question "How did the Middle Ages end?" All Julie could think of was the truth: the Middle Ages had ended when the Wild was weakened and the fairy-tale characters escaped in some grand, mysterious way that Mom never discussed.

But she couldn't write that. She had scrawled an answer about the weight of armor and the problem with plague rats in Hamlin. At the last minute, she had thrown in the word *Renaissance*.

As they turned onto Crawford Street, then West, Cindy chattered about her weekend plans—in full, gory detail, to Julie's acute embarrassment. Trying not to listen to comparisons of kissing styles, Julie focused on the road as they bounced up the hills to her house.

Mr. Wallace would read her answer out loud in class on Monday. She was sure of it. Maybe she could fake sick and stay home. Maybe she wouldn't have to fake. She felt nauseous just thinking about it. Or maybe it was Cindy's driving.

Cindy swerved into the driveway, and Julie got out quickly. "Um, thanks for the ride," she said.

"Anytime, anywhere, kiddo," Cindy said. "Remember that, next party. I'll get you home before midnight." She winked.

Julie snorted. "I'm not going to any parties. Mom barely lets me sleep over at Gillian's." Besides, at this rate, she was never even going to get invited to any.

Cindy waved her hand, bangles smacking together. "Really, anytime you need a ride, just call and I'll come. That's a royal promise. You can't break a royal promise." Blowing a kiss, Cindy sped out of the driveway. She disappeared over the hill in a cloud of exhaust.

"Gross," Julie said as she inhaled exhaust. That pretty much summed up the whole day. From sneaker to Cindy, this day was horrific. Shouldering her backpack, Julie trudged to the back door.

How could she explain she'd been distracted from class by thinking about a person who, according to all legal and historical documentation, never existed? If only she knew what had happened to him, maybe his absence wouldn't hurt so much. Today it felt as if she couldn't stop thinking about him.

She dumped her backpack and jacket on a kitchen chair. A cat leapt onto the chair and dusted her bag with his tail. She looked at him and raised her eyebrows. A fat, orange cat, he wore a brand-new, doll-sized maid's outfit. "You went to Toys 'R' Us," she said.

"Did not," the cat said. "I found it."

"Mom told you not to leave the house."

"I have slain ogres!" he said. "I have advised kings! I have frightened robbers with the beauty of my song!" Boots reared onto his back legs, cleared his throat, and swung into an off-pitch rendition of "O Sole Mio."

"Very nice," Julie said. If her father were here, would she have human brothers and sisters in addition to a five-hundred-year-old feline? Not that she didn't love her adopted brother, Boots, but it would be nice to have a sibling who could go out in public and who she could admit existed.

Mid-aria, Boots stopped singing. "Day didn't go well?" he said.

"Let me put it this way: when Gillian's mom cooks, she doesn't have to close the doors to make sure the gingerbread men don't run outside." Gillian had no idea how lucky she was.

"It could be worse," her brother said. "Look at me—how many girl cats do you think I'm likely to meet with my intelligence, wit, and fashion sense? No one told me I'd be dooming myself to the life of a lonely bachelor when we escaped the Wild. And don't even say I could date a non-talking cat." He shuddered. "It would be like you dating a chimpanzee."

Maybe it will come to that, she thought glumly—by

the time Mom allowed her to date, chimpanzees might be the only ones who didn't think she was a total freak. Julie helped herself to Oreos.

"Aren't you going to feed me?" Boots asked, curling around her ankles.

"It's not dinnertime," Julie said. "Mom said no afternoon meals."

"*You're* eating."

"It's a snack."

"I want a salmon snack."

"Okay, if you can work the can opener, you can have a salmon snack," Julie said. Her brother gave her a dirty look and, flicking his tail in the air, stalked out of the room. He ruined his dignified exit by tripping over his maid apron.

* * *

After an hour of *Simpsons* reruns, the phone rang, and Julie leaned across the couch to answer it. On the other end, Gillian said, "Was it a nightmare?"

"She didn't hit anything," Julie said. "I'd call that an improvement."

"You know, you could just borrow an Invisibility Cloak from your linen closet," Gillian said. "Cindy can't pick you up if she can't see you."

Julie sighed. She liked that Gillian was okay with the Wild, but she wished she would take it more seriously.

Gillian just didn't get that the Wild was only safe because it was small and weak. "I can't use any of the items. If I use a fairy-tale item, I could be completing a fairy-tale event. If I complete a fairy-tale event . . ."

". . . the Wild will grow," Gillian finished. "I wasn't serious. Sheesh. It wouldn't kill you to lighten up a little."

If the Wild were an ounce stronger, Mom would have locked it in the cellar instead of allowing Julie to be its keeper, no matter what happened to their plumbing. It was a responsibility, not a game. But maybe Gillian *couldn't* understand that. She wasn't Rapunzel's daughter. She didn't have the essence of fairy tales living under her bed. Julie changed the subject. "How was band?"

"Nightmare," Gillian said. "Tryouts for lead trumpet are in three weeks, and I've been practicing constantly. Or at least a lot. You know I have. But I made one teeny, tiny mistake, and Mr. Marshall accuses me of not practicing. In front of everyone! With that tone of voice he gets: 'Ms. Thomas, if you think you are too good to practice, you are sorely mistaken.'"

"Ouch," Julie said. With the phone cradled to her ear, she opened the refrigerator and rooted around for a Coke. She wished she could talk to her mom. She had tried about a zillion times in the past to ask about Dad, but Mom always sidestepped the conversation or gave half answers or promises of "when you're older."

"I said I *did* practice. And he said, 'Perhaps you should

think about practicing harder. Not all of us are naturals.' I almost died," Gillian said.

Julie found a soda. Maybe she should try to talk to Mom again. She could just ask her, point-blank, about the Wild, about their family history, about Dad . . . and she could keep asking until Mom answered, instead of letting her mom avoid the questions like usual.

"Trumpet's supposed to be what I'm good at. I can play that piece *perfectly* when I'm alone," Gillian said. "It's just when there's an audience, my lips, like, *droop*." Julie heard snaps—trumpet case snaps. Sighing to herself, Julie held the phone a few inches from her ear. She knew what was coming next.

After a few practice honks, Gillian began playing her trumpet into the phone. She missed a note and started over. Julie laid the phone on her shoulder as Gillian continued to practice. What could she say to make Mom answer this time? She could start small, like, "What was it like in the tower?" Or she could start big right away: "Why didn't Dad escape with everyone else?"

On the fifth iteration of the trumpet piece, Julie switched on the TV, volume low. She watched the flicker without paying attention to what she was seeing. Instead, she played through the conversation in her mind.

Two-thirds of the way through a *Real World* rerun, Julie heard a car in the driveway, and her heart beat faster. I could do it, she thought. I could keep pushing until Mom answers. And then I'd never have to go through another day like today. "Gotta go," she said into the phone. "Mom's home." The trumpet trilled. Louder, Julie said, "Sorry, I gotta go!" The trumpet stopped. "My mom's home."

"Call me later, okay?"

"Sure," Julie said. She hung up the phone and rubbed her ear.

Carrying groceries, Julie's mother came in the door. "Pumpkin, could you help me with the rest?" Zel called.

After the groceries, I'll begin the conversation, she promised herself. Julie went out to the car and fetched the other two grocery bags. She peeked in the top. From what she could see, her mother had bought two packages of celery and several dozen eggs. She put the bags on the kitchen table. "Couldn't we have gone out for pizza?"

"Quiche," her mom said.

"Gesundheit," Julie said.

Zel shed her coat. "It's sort of egg pie."

"Pizzas are sometimes called pizza pies," Julie said hopefully.

"I told Snow's seven to come at 6:30," Zel said.

Snow's seven! Julie groaned. She had forgotten all about the dinner party. She couldn't talk to Mom with Snow's seven coming. Mom would be busy cooking and cleaning and preparing. She would use that as an excuse to avoid any hard questions, just like every other time Julie wanted to have this conversation.

Her mother turned the oven on to preheat. "We'll have to cook in two batches. Oven's too small to hold more than two pie plates. But on the plus side," Zel said, with a quick grin at Julie, "at least we know it's never cooked a witch. Or a little German girl."

Julie plopped into a chair. She hadn't realized how much she'd wanted to talk until the chance was gone. "Why do you invite them? They're so . . ." Rude, obnoxious, condescending. ". . . sexist. Honestly, they make the Brothers Grimm look PC."

"Snow deserves a day off," her mother said. "Come on, Julie. It won't be that bad." Julie snorted. Wheedling, her mom said, "I've invited your grandmother."

"Yeah?" Julie said, feeling a grin spread across her face.

"She promised to behave this time."

Grandma was coming! At last, something to compensate for the flip-flops and the mirrors and the constant humiliation of it all: Grandma. Julie couldn't believe it. She hadn't seen her in weeks. The Wishing Well Motel was too far for an easy bike ride, and Grandma only left the motel on special occasions; she regarded it as an almost-sacred duty to personally guard the well against would-be wishers.

What had her mom said to get her to come? It couldn't

have been the quiche. Julie eyed the eggs and celery warily. She'd have a nice, safe PB&J later, she decided. "Who's watching the well?" she asked.

"The three bears," her mom said. She took a mixing bowl out of the cabinet. "Go on up and change. Anything but jeans. I don't want to hear the seven's spiel about girls in jeans."

So long as Grandma was coming, Julie would happily wear a clown suit. "Fine." Scooping up her backpack as she passed through the living room, she headed upstairs. "And put on some socks!" Zel called after her. "You'll freeze your toes in those shoes!"

Chapter Four
The Dinner Party

Julie was always surprised by the number of exceedingly short men her mother knew. All seven of their guests were short enough to rest their chins on the rims of their plates and shovel quiche directly into their mouths. Even seated, Gothel, Zel, and Julie all towered over them. If Boots were here, he and Julie would have laughed about it, but he'd pleaded other plans—he'd promised Cindy he'd help with her mouse problem.

Lucky cat.

"Girl!" one of the seven said. Didn't they know she had a name? She was Rapunzel's only daughter, and they'd known Zel for five hundred years. You'd have thought they'd bother to learn her name. "Girl," he said, "I know you haven't had the benefits of a forest education, but it's common courtesy to set the table with *clean* forks." He held up his fork, which appeared spotless to Julie, and waved it at her.

She looked at her mom. Zel mouthed, "Please."

Julie rolled her eyes and headed for the kitchen for the fifth time (not that she was counting). Zel put her hand on her wrist as she passed. "I know they're difficult," Zel whispered softly, "but they're old family friends. We owe them a lot."

Julie made a face. "They call me 'Girl,'" she whispered back.

"They called me 'Long-hair' for three centuries," Zel whispered. "Please, Julie. Just be a good hostess tonight. It won't kill you."

Old family friends—what could they possibly owe Snow's seven? She supposed it was another thing that Mom would never explain, even if Julie ever managed to ask. Julie fetched a new fork. She laid it next to the dwarf's plate and he inspected it. "There's a smudge . . ." he began.

Didn't this count as child abuse? She held out her hand for the fork and softly whistled, "Heigh-ho, heigh-ho, it's off to work . . ." Unfortunately, she didn't whistle softly enough.

"You . . . you . . . you," the dwarf sputtered. "We worked in *mines*. Hard labor!"

Julie shrank back. Uh-oh. Now she'd done it. "Sorry! I didn't mean anything."

"You didn't mean anything? You don't know anything!"

He waved the fork at her. "You don't know what it's like to be forced to work all day, knowing that someone you care about is in danger, knowing you can't protect her, knowing she will be hurt while you're gone but you *still* have to go. You don't have any choice but to go!"

Gothel plucked the fork out of the dwarf's hands, spat on the tongs, rubbed it with her napkin, and handed it back. "It's clean now," she said firmly. Quivering, he shoveled quiche in his mouth while the rest of Snow's seven stared. Gothel looked over his head at Julie and winked.

Julie sagged back in her chair. Rant averted. Score one for Grandma. Julie tried hard not to look at her mom. She'd be hearing about this later.

Breaking the awkward silence, Zel asked brightly, "So, how's the jewelry store?"

"Oh, terrible," one of them answered. "Business hasn't been the same since chain stores were invented. Frankly, I'm surprised your motel hasn't folded, Dame Gothel."

Grandma's motel, fold? Julie couldn't imagine Northboro without Grandma's motel. How could he even suggest it? Granted, the plumbing barely worked and the heat was iffy. The swimming pool hadn't held water in decades, and the rooms themselves still had the original purple-and-orange decor. (Julie's mom said it was the place 1979 went to retire.) But still, Julie loved it. She'd spent summers playing jungle in the grasses and detective in the vacated rooms. She'd caught frogs in the lobby, and she'd picked apples from the tree in the courtyard.

"The Wishing Well Motel has had guests every night for the thirty years I've run it," Gothel said, an edge in her voice. Clearly, the idea of the motel folding offended Grandma as much as it did Julie. The Wishing Well Motel was Gothel's pride and joy, Julie knew—as her mom had once explained, it let Grandma have an income and watch the well at the same time. "Dame Fortune, who has all the money that luck and the state lottery can bring, books with me," Gothel said. "Even the swimming pool is currently booked by the Giant-Ogre family for Halloween."

Obviously seizing the opportunity to shift the conversation, Zel said, "I heard they opened a Big and Tall franchise in Manhattan."

"Oh, good grief," Julie said. It sounded like a bad joke. Were these people for real? Honestly, you'd think they wanted the world to know who they were.

"Even the son?" one of the seven asked.

Julie couldn't resist: "Not him. He's trying to break into the pro-wrestling circuit, but he only wants to fight Englishmen."

"Really?" another said.

Julie rolled her eyes. "No, not really. It was a joke. 'I smell the blood of an Englishman'?"

Snow's seven didn't laugh. Some of them looked angry.

"He does interior design," Zel said, shooting her daughter a look. Julie poked at her quiche. They were all so touchy.

Gothel wasn't deterred. "Do you think I'd abandon the wishing well, even if the economy failed?" she said. "Someone has to guard it."

If Julie had the well here, she'd wish the seven were gone. Not that her grandmother would let her make that wish—or any other. Like the items in the linen closet, the wishing well was off-limits.

Once, Julie remembered, she had tried to make a wish. From her sentry point in the main office, Grandma had seen her. It was the only time Julie had witnessed her grandmother truly angry. *Do you want to feed the Wild?* she'd said. *Do you want to destroy everything?* And she had sat Julie down and proceeded to explain why the Wild was so dangerous. No one had ever done that before. For weeks after that, Julie hadn't been able to sleep in her bed for fear the Wild would trap her in one of its little puppet plays. *The Wild,* Grandma had said, *takes your free will. Every fairy-tale event that is started must be completed. Is your wish worth your freedom? Everyone's freedom?* Julie had cried. It was only a little wish, she'd lied. She'd said she wanted to wish for straight hair.

Of course, she had meant to wish for her father.

"People need that motel," Gothel said. "It's a haven for our kind."

"Our kind can't mingle too much with the non-Wild," one of the dwarves agreed. "They just don't understand. To them, we're Sneezy and Dopey. They don't understand: we didn't get a happy ending. We never got to save Snow. We worked while she died, and then we watched while some *boy* who never appreciated her carried her away."

"How can they understand?" another said. "You shouldn't blame them."

"Oh, I don't blame them," the first dwarf said. "In fact, I envy them. To have always known who you are, to be able to change who you are, to shape your fate, to make your own story . . ." He nodded at Julie in reference.

All of a sudden, everyone was looking at her. Julie shrank back. She felt her face turning bright red. She knew she wasn't like them, just like she knew she wasn't like Kristen and her flock. Did they have to point it out? Worse, did they have to point it out in her own home?

Zel cleared her throat. "Julie? Help me clear the table?"

An escape route. Thank you, Mom. Quickly, Julie collected a few of the dishes and fled into the kitchen. Following her, Zel set out the pies for dessert—berry pies, because the dwarves would not eat apple. "Honey? Are you all right?" Zel asked.

"Just great," Julie said. She turned the water on and

squeezed the soap bottle over the sink as if wringing its neck. The unfairness of it all—everything she had to go through, the secrets she had to hide, the humiliations she endured . . . and she wasn't even one of them. Her world could be ruined because of *their* secrets, and she didn't even get to be "our kind." Why did the seven have to remind her? She'd almost started to have a good time.

Gothel appeared in the doorway. "Can I help with anything, dear?"

"We have it all covered," Zel said. "Besides, I think the seven would feel better if you weren't near their dessert. It's not apple, but still, no need to upset them."

Gothel smiled but didn't argue. "In that case, may I use your phone? I told Ursa I would call after dinner."

"Please." Zel waved at the phone.

Julie scrubbed at the dinner dishes. Behind her, she heard her mother stop slicing the pies. Her mother was watching her—Julie could almost feel Mom's eyes boring into her back. "Dishes without even being asked," her mom said lightly. "I should invite Snow's seven more often."

In the other room, their sexist guests were condemning the Princess and the Pea Mattress Company commercials, in which the princess wore a low-cut nightgown. Julie scrubbed the plates savagely.

Her mom laid her hand on Julie's arm. "Julie. Honey,

talk to me. What's wrong?" Julie dunked a plate into the sink, and soapy water splashed out. Zel took a step backward as water sprayed on her. "You're going to break that plate if you're not careful," she said mildly.

"You wouldn't understand," Julie said. Mom had been in the Wild. She belonged with Grandma and Boots and Cindy and the dwarves . . . Julie was the only one who didn't fit in anywhere.

"Try me," her mom said.

For an instant, Julie was tempted. Could she have the conversation she always wanted to have? If she explained, would her mother understand? Could she know what it was like to not fit in? Could she understand what it was like to not know who she was or where she belonged? Or even where she came from? Julie knew nothing of her father. She knew nothing of how her mother and her fairy-tale friends had escaped the Wild. How was Julie even here? How had the force of the Wild Wood, a power that had dominated the entire Middle Ages, been reduced to a tangle of vines under her bed?

Behind them, Gothel hung up the phone. "Julie, be a dear and fetch my purse, would you? I left it under my chair."

Zel's voice sharpened. "What's wrong?" she asked Gothel.

Gothel's eyes flickered toward Julie.

41

"Julie," her mother said, "please go get your grand-mother's purse."

"Is it the well?" Julie asked.

"*No,*" both her mother and grandmother said in unison.

Julie swallowed a lump in her throat. "It's because I wasn't in the Wild. That's why you won't tell me. Isn't it? You know what? I don't care." She threw the sponge in the sink. "I don't care that I don't belong. I don't want to be a part of your little club."

"Julie, it's not because—" Zel began.

"I wish Grandma would let me make a wish in the well," Julie said. "I'd wish you weren't my mother."

Zel's face drained white. Gothel sucked in a breath. For a long second, the kitchen echoed silence. Her mother opened her mouth and then shut it. She looked like she'd been slapped.

Julie turned and ran from her mother's expression—out of the kitchen, through the dining room, up the stairs. She locked her bedroom door behind her and threw her-self on the bed.

The Wild left her alone as she cried herself to sleep.

Chapter Five
The Wild

Julie took a few Oreos and poured herself a glass of milk.
She was doomed to a long you-hurt-my-feelings talk. She
was just lucky that Mom worked at the salon on Saturdays
or she'd already be at the table feeling like a horrible slug
for the horrible thing she'd said to her mother.

She really, really shouldn't have said it.

Julie grabbed the whole bag of Oreos and the container
of milk and carried them into the living room. She switched
on the TV. She had six hours until Mom came home.

Cartoon, cartoon, commercial, rerun, talk show . . .
She flipped through the channels, wishing she could flip
through parts of her life like this. She imagined she was
turning her mom off, Grandma off, Kristen off, Cindy off,
the dwarves off . . . Cartoon, rerun, rerun, Torso Track
infomercial . . . *Breaking news*, she read on CNN. *Live
from Northboro, Massachusetts.* Hey, that's here!

She'd seen those Halloween decorations: the cardboard pumpkin over the Marlboro poster, the corn husk witch on the Pennzoil . . . It was the Shell gas station near Grandma's motel—or she thought it was. It didn't used to have trees between the pumps. Premium unleaded was now next to an oak tree instead of a window squeegee dispenser. Vines were twisted around the pump nozzles. Moss covered the credit card displays.

Julie leaned closer to the TV. Was that moss spreading?

" . . . *Even more alarming*," a reporter was saying, "*the rate of growth appears to be increasing.*" The TV focused on the pavement. Green (oddly vibrant for October) advanced across the blacktop like an army of worms. Tendrils snaked forward, and the asphalt cracked. Thicker vines shot into the cracks, widening the splits. The street crumbled.

Oh, no. Julie looked down at her flip-flops. She began to feel sick as a horrible suspicion solidified in her mind. No, it wasn't possible. Her door was locked. "Boots," Julie called. "Boots!"

Green seeped down a drainage hole, raced around a manhole cover, and climbed a streetlamp. The TV camera chased the vines as they braided themselves around the pole.

It was super-powered fertilizer. Yes, it had to be some escaped science experiment. Or a weird government thing, a biological weapon—but if it were a weapon, wouldn't it kill things, not make them grow?

Helicopters whirred overhead, and the reporter clutched at her coat as it fluttered around her. Gas stations did *not* just sprout trees.

"We have been told that a SWAT team has been ordered on the scene, and police are currently evacuating the surrounding area."

Boots sauntered into the living room. "Unless you found me a girlfriend, I'm going back to sleep." He froze midstride as the camera panned away from the self-service island across police cars, TV station vans, and a crowd of onlookers held back by police tape.

Looming over the crowd was a thick, dark forest.

"Oh, no," Boots said.

Julie barreled up the stairs. She grabbed the key from Mom's jewelry box, and she unlocked her bedroom door. "Please, no. Please," she said. She dropped beside her bed and yanked up the dust ruffle.

Aside from a few green stains, nothing was there.

This couldn't be happening. This couldn't be real. She'd had nightmares like this. She flopped her stomach to the floor and crawled under the bed. "Please be here. Please!"

It wasn't.

Julie wormed back out from under the bed. "No," she said. "No!" It couldn't be gone. She looked around her room—nothing under her desk, nothing behind her book-shelf. She opened her closet and shoveled clothes off the closet floor into the center of the room. She pulled the drawers out of her dresser. She searched the drawers in her desk. She ripped the covers off her bed.

Finally, there was no place left to look. She stood in the center of her wrecked room. Somehow, the Wild had escaped. Worse, it had escaped and grown. It wasn't hidden anymore.

Clapping her hands over her mouth, she ran for the bathroom. She fell in front of the toilet and retched. Government laboratories. TV documentaries. *National Enquirer* articles. Talk show specials. She'd be branded a freak forever. She'd never be able to have a normal life. The whole world would know she was Rapunzel's daughter.

Why? Why? WHY? She hadn't asked for this. She hadn't asked for a mother with secrets this big. She hadn't asked for a mother who wasn't supposed to exist.

She had, in fact, wished her mother wasn't her mother.

Stomach empty, she sank down on the bath mat. What if . . . Oh, God, could her wish have somehow caused this? Was this her fault? "No, no, no," she said. "I take it back! I didn't mean it!"

But she *had* meant it when she'd said it.

"Please, I take it back!"

How did you undo a wish? The words were out, dissolved

in the air. You couldn't suck them back in. She'd said it; it was done. And now the Wild was free . . .

No. She couldn't have caused this. She hadn't wished in the well. Just wishing aloud couldn't do anything. Hundreds, thousands, millions of people wished all the time, and their wishes didn't all come true. Look at how often she had wished for her dad. If her wishes had power, it wouldn't be just her and Mom.

Whatever had happened with the Wild, Mom would know how to fix it. Julie had to call her and tell her the Wild was free. I can't, she thought. How could she tell Mom that their worst nightmare had come true? How could she face her after what she'd said?

Knees shaking, Julie got to her feet. She splashed water on her face and rinsed her mouth. Laboratories, she reminded herself. *National Enquirer*. She had to tell Mom.

Julie went downstairs. *"As far as can be determined,"* she heard the TV say, *"it appears the growth began in the vicinity of a local establishment, the Wishing Well Motel."* She missed the last step and landed hard on the heels of her feet. Grandma . . .

She hurried to the phone and dialed the number for Rapunzel's Hair Salon.

No one answered.

Chapter Six
Behind the Yellow Tape

As Julie coasted into the parking lot of Rapunzel's Hair Salon, she heard cheesy '80s music drift out the open door. It sounded so cheerfully normal that for an instant, she thought maybe she was wrong. Maybe the Wild wasn't growing. Why would Mom be listening to the radio if the Wild was growing? She propped her bike against the bike rack and went inside. "Mom . . ." She halted beside the reception desk.

All the lights were on, and one of the dryers was blowing hot air on a vacant chair. Julie felt her heart drop into her stomach.

The salon was empty.

The salon was *never* empty.

"Mom?" Her voice came out as a squeak.

"*Oh, honey,*" she heard. The mirror! She'd forgotten the mirror! The mirror's smoke-like face drifted across the glass over Julie's reflection (frizzed hair, red sweater and jeans). *"Haven't you heard?"* the mirror said. *"The Wild Wood has returned."*

She felt dizzy. It was like there wasn't enough oxygen. Don't panic, she told herself. The fairy-tale characters stopped it before, back when the Middle Ages ended. She was sure they'd defeat it again.

Mom must have gone to watch it be defeated. She probably planned to fit it in between appointments—pop out, watch the Wild shrink; pop in, cut some bangs. That was why she hadn't bothered turning the radio off.

Julie tried to make herself believe it.

"Please, child, take me off the wall before it comes," the mirror said.

Grandma would do something witchy to defeat it. She wouldn't let the Wild recapture the fairy-tale characters or force ordinary people into its stories. Julie just had an overactive imagination.

She remembered last night when Grandma called the motel and Mom asked what was wrong. That must have been when she found out . . . But that was *before* Julie had voiced that wish. She'd been right—the Wild's escape wasn't her fault. The timing made that impossible. So why didn't that make her feel better?

Wait—if they knew about the Wild last night, then why was it still here today?

"*Smash me on the floor if you have to,*" the mirror said, "*but don't leave me here. I will not lose myself again. I cannot.*"

Something was wrong. Something was terribly wrong, and the mirror knew it.

Julie's feet were moving under her, faster and faster. She ran out of the salon, down the steps, and to her bike. Getting on, she started pedaling.

Grandma will stop it, she told herself. It'll be okay. It had to be okay.

She heard sirens. Outside Shattuck's Pharmacy, she saw the ABC Channel 5 News van, and her heart jumped into her throat. She tried to calm herself: she'd seen this on the news, so of course there were news vans. It didn't mean anything. It didn't mean the Wild was still growing. Please, don't be growing.

In the distance, she heard the thrum of a helicopter. She passed more news vans and then emergency vehicles: police cars, ambulances, fire engines. Red siren lights splashed across the buildings. It's okay, she repeated, Grandma will fix it; it's all okay.

She came around the corner of the library, and she saw the crowd: a teeming swarm of reporters, scientists, and police. On TV, the crowd hadn't looked so large. Or so upset. Why were there so many people? What did it mean that there were so many people? Where was Mom? Where was Grandma?

Grandma should be vanquishing the Wild—it should be writhing and melting into a puddle of vines. Or whatever it did. Standing on her toes on the pedals, Julie looked for the Wild.

Above the street and beyond the crowd, she saw dark summer green where there should have been bare autumn branches. It was a smear of dark green. A big smear. A very, very big smear. She realized she was gripping the handlebars of her bike so hard that it hurt. *This* had been under her bed? It wasn't possible. It was so . . . *big*.

How could Grandma, or anyone, stop it?

Julie ditched her bike at the library and plunged into the crowd. "Mom? Mom!" Instantly, she lost sight of the forest as the crowd swarmed around her. Armpit level with the adults, she wormed between jackets and coats. "'Scuze me. Excuse me!" People surged around her, and she was swept forward.

Hundreds of camera shutters clicked. Police yelled into megaphones: "*Stand away from the tape. Behind the yellow tape. Stand away from the tape.*" A film crew muscled past her. Grabbing the back of a flannel shirt, she followed in their wake.

Someone pushed into her, and she lost her grip. She fell into the yellow police tape. She lifted her eyes, and for the first time, the Wild was directly in front of her. Only three feet of pavement separated her and the trees.

Gnarled limbs stretched like frozen fingers. Trunks curved into mouthlike holes. Julie froze, a deer in headlights. It'll eat me, she thought. If it catches me, it'll eat me.

She saw remnants of the Shell station laced in leaves. Thick, ancient-looking oaks enveloped the structure. Only the UNLEADED price sign and bits of roof were visible now. It looked much, much worse in person than it had on TV. She stared at the sign and thought of the way the Wild had consumed her sneaker. What if her mom were in there, wrapped in trees? Don't think that! Her mom wasn't in there. She was safe. She was fine. Any second, Julie would see her in the crowd, and . . .

A loud whir grew behind her.

She turned and saw a military helicopter flying low over Main Street. *We have been told that a SWAT team has been ordered on the scene,* she remembered. Julie clapped her hands over her ears as the copter rumbled and whined. Her eyes (and those of everyone in the crowd) followed the dark gray helicopter as it flew over their heads and over the top of the encroaching forest.

"No," Julie whispered—my sneaker, she thought. She had thrown her sneaker at the Wild, and the Wild had swallowed it. They were throwing a helicopter . . . Oh, no. No, no. "Wait! Don't!"

As soon as the rear of the helicopter crossed over the invisible line between ordinary street and the Wild, it happened: the Wild, like some kind of gigantic octopus, flung thick vines into the air—the crowd gasped—Julie couldn't breathe. The vines wrapped around the helicopter—the blades stopped. Suddenly, there was silence, and then the vines pulled the helicopter down into the forest. "No," she said.

She heard a horrible crunching noise—metal being crushed.

And the crowd started to scream.

Julie shoved through the mob. "Mom! MOM!" She was thrown back into the police tape. "Mommy! Zel! Rapunzel!"

Half the people tried to flee, and the other half surged forward. Julie clung to the yellow tape as people knocked into her. *"Please keep calm . . ."* a voice on a megaphone said. "Oh, we're going to die!" someone wailed. "We're all going to die!" Another shouted, "Call in the army! Blow it to bits!" ". . . *an orderly evacuation,*" the megaphone said. Evacuation? No, she couldn't leave. Not before she found Mom!

"Idiots!" she heard, shrill over the crowd. "Numskulls! I told you not to enter it! It will trap you if you enter it! Fools!"

She recognized the voice: Goldilocks. It felt like a lifeline in a storm. Goldie, Mom's friend. "Goldie!" Julie called. She waved her arms in the air. "Goldie, over here!"

Julie tried to push toward her, but the tide of the crowd swept against her as police corralled the onlookers back. Elbows and arms jabbed into her. "No! Let me through!" Julie squirmed through the press of people. She burst out in front. The woods, huge and dark, rose up in front of her. She jumped back from the leading edge of moss, and the crowd again swallowed her.

She didn't see Goldie. Where was she? Julie spun in a circle and saw a flash of pink Lycra. "Cindy!" she cried.

"Oh, Julie!" Cindy pushed toward her and crushed her in a hug.

Julie shoved back from her. "Cindy, where is she?" Tears clogged her eyes. She wiped them back. She had to see. She had to find Mom! "Where is she! Where's my mom?"

"You shouldn't be here," Cindy said. "Let me take you to safety. We can get in my car and drive. All the way to California if we have to."

She choked down panic. "But where's—"

Cindy squeezed Julie's shoulders. "Julie, honey, sweetheart . . ." Leaning in so Julie could hear her, Cindy shouted in Julie's ear, "Your mother was a hero! She got the motel guests away before any of them realized what was happening!"

Julie didn't understand. Her mother wasn't a hero; her mother was a hairdresser. What did Cindy mean, "she got the motel guests away"? What did she mean, "was a hero"? What did she mean "*was*"? Julie gulped in air. Her heart was thudding in her ears, louder than the shouting. "What . . ." Her voice squeaked. She licked her lips and tried again: "What do you mean?"

Shoving a rubbernecker aside, Goldie strode toward them. "You! It's your mother's fault! She made it worse! It doubled in size after she went in and joined its stories." Cindy hissed at her, but Goldie shook her ringlets viciously and continued, "She *had* to be the hero. Always the hero! Never thinking about *me*!"

After she went in? Mom went in? In the Wild? In that *thing* that ate a police helicopter? Her mom was in *that*? The thick vines were strangling the gas station sign, and the station's roof was now completely obscured by dense, dark leaves. "*Get back from the yellow tape!*" the megaphones blared. Julie started to shake. She had to have heard wrong. Film crews pushed past her. The shouting was a buzz in her ears. "But . . . what . . ." She turned to Cindy.

"She went in after Gothel," Cindy said, pity in her eyes.

Julie gaped at her. Grandma was in there too? Mom and Grandma were in the Wild? No. It was too much. It couldn't be happening. It had to be some horrible nightmare. Wake up, Julie. Please, wake up. She felt tears on her cheeks. She wiped her nose with her sleeve.

"Oh, honey," Cindy said. "Let me take you away from here." She put her arm around Julie and tried to guide her away.

Julie didn't move. Mom *and* Grandma . . . Feeling sick, she looked up at the tangled green. A hundred feet above the street, the leaves clawed the sky—was it wind, or were they moving on their own? Oh, please, she thought, let this not be happening. Why was this happening? She thought again of her wish. "Last night, I wished . . . I wished . . ."

Goldie drew herself taller. "You stupid girl! You idiotic—" Her hands curled into fists, and her arms shook.

"You wished in the well?" Cindy said.

"No!" Julie said. "But I wished out loud . . ." Again, she saw the look on Mom's face. Julie's throat clogged. She couldn't repeat what she'd said.

"Oh, sweetie, that couldn't have done it," Cindy said. "Only a wish in the well could do this. While Gothel was at your house last night, someone had to have snuck in to the well and wished for the Wild to be at the motel, free and strong. It was not your fault. You couldn't have caused this."

Cindy was right—Julie hadn't been near the well, and she didn't have any magic powers. But that didn't make her feel any better. Julie flinched as a camera flashed in her eyes. The flash failed to illuminate the shadows of the Wild. Dark and silent, the woods towered over the crowd.

Someone had wished for the Wild to escape and grow. Someone had caused this to happen to Mom and Grandma. Who would do that? "But . . . but . . . who? Why?"

Cindy wrung her hands. "We don't know!"

"I hope the Wild caught them," Goldie said. "I hope it makes them dance to death in iron shoes. Again and again. Or burn in their own oven. Or plummet from a cliff . . ."

The pavement trembled under them, and Julie heard a crunch as a length of sidewalk split under the pressure of the green. New tendrils shot across the yellow police tape. "Someone has to do something," Julie said.

"Run," Goldie suggested.

"Someone has to stop it. Someone has to save them." She scanned the crowd. People were scattering like chickens, running in frantic circles. "The police . . ."

". . . have no idea what they're dealing with," Goldie said scornfully. "You could nuke it, and it would transform the nuke. The police can't stop it."

"Someone who knows the Wild, then. One of the heroes," Julie said. "Or a magician. Or a fairy." She latched onto Cindy. "You have a fairy godmother. Call her!" Cindy began to shake her head sadly. "Fairy godmother!" Julie shouted. "Please, fairy godmother! I need you! Fairy godmother!"

Pop.

Smoke puffed in front of them, and Julie sneezed. She opened her eyes to see a plump woman in a bathing suit and butterfly wings standing in front of her. All the TV cameras swung toward them. The fairy lowered her sunglasses on her nose. "Oh, my goodness," she said, "it has been an age. Don't you know I'm retired? I don't do balls anymore."

"Please," Julie said. Her throat stuck. Her face felt hot. She couldn't talk. Her mother . . . Mom was in the Wild.

"Can you take her to safety?" Cindy asked the fairy.

The fairy saw the forest, and she blanched. "Oh, oh! How terrible! This was such a nice country!" Her wings fluttered agitatedly, and she rose up onto her toes. "How did this happen?"

"Stupid well," Goldie said. "We should have buried it in cement. We should've hidden it behind barbed wire and laser sensors—"

"The child," Cindy reminded the fairy.

Instantly, the fairy godmother smiled, falsely bright, at Julie. "Don't worry, my dear. We can be in Florida in an eyeblink. Or maybe Europe. Yes, you'll be safe from the Wild there, for a time. Oh, who could have done such a thing? Who would want the Wild to come back?"

"No, no," Julie wailed. "You have to stop it! You have to save my mother! Wave your wand and fix it!" She waved her hands at the towering trees.

"Me? Oh, no, dear. I can't stop the Wild from the outside. No one can. Just like no one could destroy the wishing well. Or even change your mother's hair color. It can't be done."

Why didn't they want to help her? This was her mother, their friend! What was wrong with them? "Then go *inside*!"

All three of them seemed shocked. "Oh, I couldn't," the fairy godmother said. "Are you crazy?" Goldie shrieked. "We have to keep people out!" "Oh, sweetie," Cindy said, "you don't understand. If we went in there, we'd be back in the stories."

"You can't resist it," the fairy godmother said. "If you find a bear's house, you must eat their porridge. If you go to a ball, you must lose a slipper. It would be worse for us: we have roles. The Wild knows which set of events would suit us best, and it would ensure we found them. It would catch us quickly."

"But you escaped before!" Julie cried. "You stopped it before!"

"*We* didn't," Goldie said, harsh. "Why do you think the Wild was in your house? Your mother was the only one who knew how to stop it—that's why she was responsible for guarding it. She wasn't supposed to let this happen. She swore this would never happen." Goldie buried her face in her hands. "I can't go back there! I can't! You don't know what it's like in there—I have no home, no friends, no family. I'm hungry. I'm tired. I'm cold. When

Snow's lost in the woods, the dwarves welcome her in. They love her. Me, I'm chased by bears! And there's no reprieve, always chased, always hated . . ."

Cindy put her arm around her, and Goldie knocked it away.

Mom was the only one who knew how to stop it? Julie's stomach flopped and, despite her sweater and the bike ride, she felt cold. Mom? Julie looked to Cindy. Was this true? No one else knew how to stop it? But . . . why? Why would her mother be the only one who knew?

Cindy wrung her hands. "Your parents were alone, and your mother never liked to talk about it." Julie stared at her. What was she saying? Her parents were alone when the Wild was defeated . . . her parents were part of its defeat? "We didn't press her," Cindy said. "She never got over losing your father, you know. She still misses him."

"But . . ." Julie said. She didn't understand. She didn't want to understand. Her father was there when the Wild was defeated . . .

"Your father died in there," Goldie said. "He died getting us out."

Holding out her hand, the fairy godmother forced a smile. "Come on, pumpkin. Take my hand." *Pumpkin.* Mom always called her "pumpkin."

Julie turned and ran into the crowd.

Chapter Seven
Linda the Librarian

Julie ducked into the library and collapsed against the book return box. Leaning around the box, she peeked out through the glass door. She didn't see anyone on the sidewalk. Several policemen hurried by on the street. A squad car drove off in the opposite direction. She'd lost them. She was alone.

She suddenly realized how true that was. I *am* alone, she thought. Mom's in the Wild, and I'm alone. Julie felt sick. Putting her head between her knees, she tried to take deep breaths. Cindy and Goldie wouldn't—or couldn't—help. And Mom and Grandma were in the Wild. In the Wild!

Your father died in there. He died getting us out. But how? Why such secrets? Why such terrible secrets? What had happened?

Shouldn't someone know? Shouldn't there be a story?

Wasn't that the way Mom had said it worked? Anything that happened in the Wild became a story in the real world, she'd said. So shouldn't there be some book with the tale of their escape?

And wasn't she in a library?

Julie jumped to her feet and ran to the children's room. The librarian, Linda, smiled and waved at her as she came in. "Julie! How nice to see you," she said.

Julie knew the exact shelf, the one beside the cage with the pet mice. She used to spend hours here, poring through every version of *Rapunzel* for hints of her father. In their cage, the three mice pressed their noses to the glass as Julie ran her fingers over the book spines. *Bluebeard, Six Swans, Cinderella, Frog Prince, Snow White* . . . It wouldn't be in a traditional tale or she would have seen it before. It had to be part of an obscure tale, bundled in a collection. And it would be unique. Unlike other events in the Wild, the defeat of the Wild could only have happened once. There wouldn't be hundreds of variations.

Julie pulled out anthologies of Perrault, Hans Christian Andersen, Jack Zipes, and Asbjornsen and Moe. She dropped down to the floor and opened them one by one. How to win a kingdom, how to defeat a dragon, how to annoy a fairy, how to please elves, how to do impossible tasks, how to rescue a princess . . .

Julie sprang up and pulled out the Andrew Lang

fairy-tale books one by one. She flipped to the end of each tale. "Marriage, marriage, death, marriage . . ." She tossed the books on the floor as she finished with them.

Smile wavering, Linda picked up the books as they hit the floor. "Can I help you find something?"

"Aren't there any more?" Julie asked. She took *The Complete Grimm's Fairy Tales* off the shelf. Rapunzel appeared in only one story, the traditional tower story. It ended with Rapunzel wandering the desert until she found her prince, then crying to cure his blindness. Julie flipped pages. Nothing after "happily ever after." Nothing about how she had escaped the Wild, reconciled with Gothel, and delayed Julie's birth until she deemed it safe. Not even a hint. Julie snapped the book closed. "I need a story about the fairy-tale characters escaping the fairy tale," Julie said.

"Oh," Linda said. "It's out."

"*Out?*" Julie said, astounded. It actually existed, and the library owned a copy? How had she never seen it here before? How had she never read it? A book with all the answers she'd ever wanted! Just thinking about it made her head spin.

"And so are the interlibrary loan copies and the copies in the Worcester Library," Linda said. She headed for the circulation desk. "You won't find it in Boston either." Julie didn't think to question how Linda knew about the other libraries' copies.

Oh, Mom, why didn't you tell me? Why didn't you tell anyone?

Outside, the police sirens screamed. *"An emergency evacuation is in effect,"* the megaphone blared. "Some might say," Linda said softly, under the sound of the sirens, "this may not be such a horrible thing. With all the new people inside, there are bound to be new tales born out of the old stories. And the world needs new fairy tales. Or so some might say."

Julie didn't hear her. She stared at the cover of *Grimm's*: a painting of a princess, a knight, a tower, and a frog. Did it matter that no one else knew? So long as Mom knew how to stop it, that was enough, wasn't it?

If it was enough, why hadn't she already escaped? Something must have prevented her: wolves, ogres, witches. She imagined her mother tied to a stake, a dragon circling above. Mom wouldn't put up with it: she'd send the dragon to its room and cancel all its chocolate privileges. Julie half laughed, half hiccuped. No, no, she would not get hysterical.

But that had to be the reason why Mom wasn't here right now: something had caught her before she could act, and she was a prisoner somewhere. Julie traced the image of the tower on the cover of the book. Rescues happened all the time in the Wild. She'd seen a dozen tales just now. All Mom needed was to be rescued, and then she could do the rest.

Julie just had to call a hero, and it would all be fixed. Yes, that was it! "Can I use the library phone?" she asked.

Linda's forehead puckered in a frown. "The library phone is not for personal use . . ."

"Don't you hear the sirens? This is an emergency! I need to call heroes!"

Linda began to smile. "Ah, yes. The new generation of tales do need heroes. Please, be my guest . . ."

Julie hurried past her. She picked up the phone at the circulation desk. She tried to remember the heroes' real-world names: Jack the Giant Killer was Jack Bean; Prince Charming was Philip Charmin . . . None of the heroes lived in Northboro. Not enough adventure here, her mother had said. Some were in New York, some in L.A., and at least one was hunting yeti in the Himalayas. But they'd come back once they knew. Of course they would.

She dialed.

"*What city?*" the computer voice said. "New York," Julie said. She wiped her free hand on her jeans. She was sweating. "*What name?*"

"Jack Bean. *B-e-a-n.*"

She'd start with hello, how are you. She'd say she had a problem. No, she'd flatter him first: she'd say she'd heard how brave a hero he was, and then she'd tell him about the Wild and Mom. She dialed his number, and the phone rang.

She heard a click, and her heart leapt. "*Jack and the*

Giantess aren't in right now," a woman's voice boomed. A younger male voice continued: *"But if you'd like to leave a message, please wait for the 'moo.'"* On cue, a cow mooed.

He wasn't home? How could he not be home? She left a message, and then she tried Prince Charming: Philip Charmin in L.A. Another answering machine.

So far, she was batting zero, and it was getting harder and harder to stay calm. Who else could she call? She didn't know Aladdin's last name. He was a test pilot in the air force. Pinocchio wasn't much of a hero—he'd been a child actor for the past fifty years. The mattress princess's husband was in Europe somewhere. The Frog Prince was a nature specialist in the Okefenokee Swamp. Julie had never met Snow's ex-husband, and Rose (a.k.a. Sleeping Beauty) never even talked about hers. As for the others— the simpleton heroes, the lucky third sons, the invisible princes—Julie didn't know if they were in the United States or Europe, or even if they'd ever escaped from the Wild in the first place. She certainly didn't know their names, real or fairy tale. Her head felt as if it were buzzing. Julie's plan was falling apart before it had even begun. She made herself put the receiver down on the cradle. Abruptly, the buzzing stopped.

There had to be some way she could find out their real-world names. Cindy and Goldie would know, of course, but she couldn't go back to them. Who else . . .

Boots! Yes! Boots would know!

She ran around the circulation desk. "Thank you!" she called to Linda.

"You're welcome," Linda said. She still had an odd smile on her face. Julie didn't have time to think about what it meant. And she didn't see Linda walk back to the mouse cage and set the Three Blind Mice free. "You're very welcome."

Chapter Eight
Alone

Julie coasted into her driveway as the garage door lurched, closing. Mom was home! Cindy was wrong! Looking for Mom's car, she stood up on the pedals.

A fat orange cat scooted out tail-first under the closing garage door. She swallowed back disappointment. It wasn't Mom; it was Boots.

Did Boots know about Mom? Oh, how was she going to tell him? He was not going to take this well. "Boots?" Julie said.

Boots jumped and turned. "You're home!"

"Listen, Boots . . ." She looked down at the pavement and blinked fast. Why did she feel like crying again? Why was it so hard to say? "Boots, Mom's in the Wild."

He didn't say anything—he's in shock, she thought. Julie raised her head. "Boots, I need to call . . ." she began. She stopped. He was wearing his cloak and boots. He had a sack over his shoulder. Boots never wore clothes outside the house. "Are you running away?" she asked.

He ducked his head. "Not exactly."

She had a horrible thought. "Are you running *toward?*"

"You don't understand my kind of loneliness," he said. "I am the only talking cat in the real world. I'll never find love outside the Wild."

Julie felt as if the pavement had been ripped from under her feet. Speechless, she stared at him. First her mom and Grandma, and now Boots. She was losing her family. She shook her head—maybe she'd misunderstood. "You don't mean . . ."

"Plus there's the constant fear of being tossed into some evil government laboratory where I'll be dissected into a zillion pieces." He said it casually, but he shuddered all the way down to the tip of his tail. "If I can avoid any poor miller's sons, I might be able to stay free of my story, find my dream girl-cat, and start a new life. The Wild will be a jumble while it's growing. I should be able to pick and choose my own tale or even avoid the tales altogether. It won't be the same as last time."

She didn't understand. "You aren't happy here?" A dozen memories jumped into her mind: hide-and-seek (he always hid in the cat food cabinet) and cards (he always demanded they play Go Fish). Sure, they weren't always buddy-buddy. But brothers and sisters were supposed to fight and tease. She'd never meant anything by it. And she'd never thought it was serious enough to make him want to leave. "Is it me?"

He wouldn't meet her eyes. "It isn't you," he said. "I just don't belong here."

"Of course you belong. You're my brother!"

He flinched but said, "I'm a cat. A five-hundred-plus-year-old talking cat who eats Fancy Feast and pretends to chase squirrels so strangers will think I'm a pet."

But . . . but she'd grown up with him. Maybe she wasn't from the Wild. Maybe she didn't know what it had been like outside the Wild for all those years, but he'd been her brother for every year she had been alive. That wasn't something you could toss away like it didn't mean anything. "We're family. We have to stick together." You couldn't just stop being family. She gulped and blinked, trying not to cry. "Mom needs us."

"Your mother had some money in her jewelry box. You can use it for a bus from the center of Shrewsbury. If you start now, you should be able to outdistance the Wild. For a little while, at least."

How could he do this? Bad enough that the Wild had escaped and Mom and Grandma were lost—how could Boots deliberately abandon her? How could he reject her? They were family, whether he liked it or not. "What about family loyalty? Are you just going to abandon your own sister?" Despite her best efforts, her voice cracked. "Did you plan this? Did you make the wish in the well?"

"Of course not—Zel would skin me alive," he said. "But I'm not going to cry over spilt milk either. I have a second chance—the love of my life could be in there."

That was the most selfish, the most . . .

Dropping to four paws, he ran down the driveway. "I'm sorry, Julie!"

"You are the worst brother ever!" she called after him. "You're not a cat; you're a rat!" She chased him to the end of the driveway. "Come back! Boots!"

Brim of his hat bobbing, he only ran faster, disappearing over the hill without looking back. She hugged herself against the October air. Alone, she trudged inside.

The house felt very empty. The hum of the refrigerator was extra loud, like an overgrown mosquito. She heard the living room clock tick. Julie didn't like the thoughts she was thinking. She didn't like the feeling in her stomach, as if she were hanging upside down. She didn't like the horrible whisper in her head: *What if they're right? What if all she could do was run?*

Julie climbed the stairs slowly. Going into her mother's bedroom, she lifted the lid of her mother's jewelry box. Potpourri smells wafted out of it, and Julie swallowed a lump in her throat. Her mother loved "smell-good stuff," as she called it—anything but rose or pine or forest-scented. Her jewelry box smelled a little like jam.

The money that Boots had mentioned was on top, a stack of folded twenties. She could take a bus from the center of Shrewsbury to New York and from there, any-where.

Julie picked up the bills. Underneath them were her mother's necklaces. Julie set the money aside and looked through them: the jade circle that the Nightingale had given her, the cat pendant shaped like Boots, the silver choker the dwarves had made. She held the choker in her hands, remembering how many times she'd seen it around her mother's neck. She pictured her mom looking like a movie star in her black floor-length dress and this neck-lace. She had worn that outfit to Julie's fifth-grade play, saying it was Julie's premiere, so she should dress the part. Julie blinked fast.

Reaching back into the box, her fingers brushed her mom's key. All the times that her mother had reminded her to lock her bedroom door hadn't mattered at all. Even if she'd piled on locks, the Wild still would have been whisked to freedom. It had escaped through a wish, not through doors.

Cindy had said it wasn't Julie's wish. It couldn't have been. Grandma had called Ursa at the motel *before* Julie had said that horrible thing. Something had happened at the motel before Julie ever spoke. But even though her wish hadn't caused this, she still felt responsible. The Wild had been under her bed, after all.

Julie tried to remember if she had seen the Wild last night when she went to bed, and she couldn't remember actually looking. She had assumed it was there. She should have checked. If she'd checked, if she'd known sooner . . . But no, she'd been too busy feeling sorry for herself.

It hit her like a blow: what if her wish—her horrible wish that Zel weren't her mother—were the last thing she ever said to her?

Thinking about it made her insides twist. It didn't matter that her wish hadn't caused the Wild to escape, she realized. What mattered was that she'd said it at all. Mom was now trapped in the Wild thinking that Julie hated her, and Julie might never have the chance to explain. She kept replaying the night in her head. What if she never saw her mother again, never heard her say "uppy snuppy" again, never laughed at her horrible quiche again? What if that was the last moment she got?

She couldn't let that happen. If no one would go in to rescue Mom, she'd go herself. The thought made her catch her breath. Could she . . . No, no, it was crazy. She wasn't a hero. The idea of voluntarily entering the woods with all its dragons, witches, and ogres . . . Julie shuddered. It was a job for a hero. Like my father, she thought.

He died in there. Her hands clenched. The Wild killed her father, and now it had her mother.

The Wild has declared war on your family, she thought. Now, what are you going to do about it?

"Stupid," she said out loud. How could she go up against the Wild? She was one girl. She had nothing to help her make it through the Wild . . .

Or did she? Dropping the necklaces, she picked up Mom's special key—the key that opened all locks, including the linen closet.

Chapter Nine
The Linen Closet

If this was a war, here was her arsenal.

What should she take? What did heroes use against witches, wolves, ogres, magicians . . . ? She'd better take everything.

Julie inhaled deeply, then plunged into the closet and began shoveling items into her backpack: wands, hats, scarves, small boxes. Into a side pocket, she dumped a handful of magic rings. She added a jeweled knife, a table-cloth, several feathers, and a purse with pebbles. Shelf by shelf, she emptied the closet and stuffed the backpack until it was bursting.

When she finished with the shelves, she knelt down and sorted through the boots on the floor—too small, too large, too incomplete . . . She extracted a pair of brown boots and examined them. They looked like they would fit, and (except for a frayed lace) they were mostly whole.

Julie flipped off her left sandal and put on a boot. Holding on to the linen closet door, she stood up on her other foot. Carefully, she placed the boot down. With a whoosh of air, she found her nose pressed against the wall.

Ouch.

Guess it works, she thought. Balancing, she took off the boot. With the magic Seven League Boots, she felt much better. They could help her cross the forest in seconds. She'd tie them to the handlebars of her bike, she decided, and she'd put them on as soon as she entered the Wild. With luck, she'd be in and out of the woods before the Wild could trap her in any of its stories.

In and out of the woods.

This, she thought, is a terrible idea. What was she doing? She couldn't do this. She couldn't walk into the Wild and intentionally use fairy-tale items. She'd only be making things worse. It was stupid to take this stuff. Using it could set off fairy-tale events. Using it could trap her in a story. Using it could make the Wild grow larger faster. It went against everything Mom had ever taught her. Mom would have a fit if she knew Julie was even thinking about doing it.

On the other hand, did she really want to waltz into the Wild empty-handed?

Standing on tiptoes, she felt along the upper shelves. Her fingers brushed cool metal. She pulled the item down.

It was a trumpet. Gillian, she thought. I have to warn Gillian! By now, the Wild could be at Crawford Street. Julie dumped out some scarves and hats and crammed the trumpet into her pack. She zipped it shut, then locked the closet door. After a moment's thought, she slipped the works-on-any-door key into her jeans pocket. She hurried to the phone.

Busy signal.

That meant someone was still home.

Stop there first, Julie decided, and then into the Wild. With luck, Gillian would talk her out of going at all.

* * *

Distantly, Julie heard sirens. She knocked on Gillian's door. "Gillian!" She rang the bell. "Gillian! Mrs. Thomas!" She pounded with her fist.

She heard shouting inside, then footsteps. Gillian yanked open the door. "Julie!" Behind her, Gillian's five-year-old sister, Rachel, screamed, "Not without my Barbies!" Her mother boomed back: "You are getting in that car, young lady, whether I have to carry you there or not! Now, let go of that table!"

"Did you hear?" Gillian said to Julie. "Police are evacuating the street. News says they've called out the National Guard. No one knows what's going on, but it's big." Rachel shrieked like an irate dolphin, and both

77

Gillian and Julie winced. "Sirens freaked her out," Gillian said. "It's like a national disaster or something. In Northboro! Can you believe it? I mean, nothing ever happens here. There's this, like, monster growth—"

Julie interrupted, "It's the Wild."

Gillian's mouth pursed into a small o.

"It's got my mom," Julie said.

Gillian's mouth opened and shut, wordless.

Trying to sound braver than she felt, Julie said, "I'm going in." She was not going to let Gillian talk her out of it. No matter what she said. She was going to be strong and . . .

"Oh, wow," Gillian said. "Can I go?"

Julie gawked at her. "No."

"C'mon," she said. "You can't leave me out of this. Nothing this interesting ever happens to me. I want to save the day too."

Was Gillian really saying this? Didn't she understand how serious this was? Didn't she get how dangerous the Wild was? "No!"

"We'll get to have adventures. Real adventures," Gillian said. Poking Julie's arm, she waggled her eyebrows. "Princess adventures."

"It's got my *mom*," Julie said, glaring at her. This wasn't a game. Last time the Wild was this strong, it had kept her mother and her mother's friends prisoner for centuries, forcing them to reenact their fairy tales over and over, century after century. Whatever happened there had been so traumatic that none of them ever spoke about how they'd escaped—not even, apparently, to each other.

Gillian shot a look over her shoulder and then leaned in conspiratorially. "So what's the plan? How are we going to get in?"

Julie felt like tearing her hair out. "I could *die*. Eaten by ogres. Broiled by witches. Thrown into barrels with sharp nails. Fairy tales aren't jokes. Happily ever after is only at the very end—and only for the heroes and princesses."

For an instant, Julie thought she'd gotten through to her. Gillian swallowed hard. But then she rallied and said, "Gee, you couldn't be a little more optimistic?"

Julie turned her bike around. "I'm going," she said.

"Wait, I'll get my bike." Gillian ran to her garage, and Julie started riding down the brick walk. Her backpack bounced on her back. Broiled by witches, Julie thought. Barrels with nails. She wished she hadn't thought of that. Whatever Gillian believed of the Wild, Julie knew the truth: it wasn't nice.

Gillian's mother appeared in the doorway. "Girls! Oh, patience! Don't do this to me!" Rachel swung from her arm, shouting up at her. Her mother yelled, "Julie, you come back here or I'm calling your mother!" Gillian wheeled her bike out of the garage. Her mother caught sight of her. "Gillian, get back here! This instant! Gillian!" Gillian, following Julie, bounced across the lawn.

Rachel pulled on her mother's pants. "If she doesn't have to go, I don't have to!"

Her mother herded her toward their car. "In, in! We'll catch her!" She sat in the driver's seat. "Keys!" She ran back into the house.

Sirens wailed as a police car turned down Crawford Street. "*An emergency evacuation is in effect. Repeat: an emergency evacuation is in effect.*" Julie and Gillian leaned into their handlebars and pedaled faster. The boots smacked against Julie's bike frame.

Swerving left onto West Street, they sailed down the hill. At the bottom of the hill, the street turned and the Wild was suddenly in front of them. Both Julie and Gillian squeezed their brakes. The bikes tipped forward, and they caught their balance with their feet. "Wow," Gillian said. "I didn't think it would be so *big*."

Julie had known it was big. She hadn't expected it to be guarded.

The forest marched up the street toward them. Lions, tigers, bears, and wild boar prowled the perimeter. "Julie, they're walking on their hind feet," Gillian said, her voice shrill. "Those aren't normal animals."

"Thank you, Sherlock," Julie said. She felt like an idiot. She should have realized the fairy-tale characters would post guards to stop people from entering and feeding the Wild—it was the logical next step after Cindy and Goldie failed to convince people with words.

"They're . . ." Weird, disgusting, incredibly scary, Julie thought. ". . . *amazing*," Gillian said. Amazing? Was she not looking at the same army of animals Julie was looking at?

Lowering his tusks, a boar spit in their direction. A grizzly reared onto his hind legs and pounded his chest. Six trolls marched in front of them. Julie swallowed. Her throat felt like sand. How were they going to get past them? Some hero she was if she couldn't even enter the woods.

"I think I see a unicorn," Gillian said. She sounded starstruck.

"Watch the horn. He has a temper." Julie shed her backpack and rummaged through it. Something in here had to help. First to come out was the trumpet. Gillian picked it up. "Oh, wow, what's this?"

Did she have to sound like it was Christmas? She wasn't helping. Julie pulled out a wand and shook it at the guards. Flowers spewed from its tip. She tossed it away. Pulling out a box, she opened it. It held donuts. She closed it and opened it again. This time, it held éclairs.

Gillian lifted the trumpet to her lips and puffed out her cheeks. A lion, walking upright and wearing a crown, snarled at her. Gillian squeaked a note. The trolls clapped their hands over their ears. One of the bears huffed.

"Quit playing around," Julie said, exasperated.

"One more try," Gillian said. Julie blinked at her. She sounded determined. Maybe she *did* understand how serious this was. Maybe her enthusiasm was her way of being brave—Julie hadn't thought of that before. Adjusting her lips on the mouthpiece, Gillian tried again. This time, she blew a long, clear note.

Snarls died. She played a scale, stumbling over the middle notes. One of the wild boars sat down, transfixed. Smiling, the trolls leaned against each other. Gillian grinned. "They like me!" she said happily.

"Keep going," Julie whispered. Did she dare hope?

Gillian plunged into the school fight song.

The animals began to dance.

"I'll—keep—them—dancing," Gillian said between notes. "You—go—for—it!" Swinging her backpack over her shoulder, Julie got on her bike. She hesitated for a second. Should she leave Gillian here? Would she be safe? What if the Wild advanced?

Wait, did this mean Julie would have to go in alone? Suddenly, she didn't want to do that. She couldn't do this by herself! Gillian had to come with her!

Finishing the song, Gillian held out her pinky. "Luck," she said. Automatically, Julie shook her pinky with her own. Gillian inhaled again and launched into "Be Kind to Your Web-Footed Friends." The lions and the bears linked arms and skipped in circles with the trolls. Lowering her head like a charging bull, Julie pedaled between the dancing animals and rode off the pavement into the green.

Part Two

The Tower

Chapter Ten
Into the Woods

Pine needles crunched under the bike wheels as Julie pedaled over the path. She looked back over her shoulder at the world outside the Wild: streets and sunlight, dancing bears and Gillian. She could hear a Strauss march and police sirens mixed up with troll grunts and the stamping of hooves. Gillian had done it! She'd saved the day. She'd gotten Julie safe inside the Wild.

Underneath her, her Schwinn ten-speed neighed.

"Hey!" Julie clutched the handlebars as the front wheel lifted in the air. Wheel twisting, the bike shook its handles as if shaking a mane. "Stop it! Who's doing . . ." The bike lurched, and Julie tumbled off the seat and landed smack on the pine needle floor.

Flashing its front reflector back at her, the bike hopped over roots, and she forgot about the pain of the fall. Oh, wow. Her bike was alive. She had a living bike.

Oh, no. Her bike was alive. Pedals spinning on their own, the bike (with her magic boots still tied to it) sped off into the forest. "Wait! Come back!" She scrambled to her feet and ran after it. It dodged between the trees, and she stumbled as her sandal caught on a root. Catching herself on a tree trunk, she called after it, "Bike, come back!" It disappeared between the trees.

Ferns folded like closing curtains to hide the bike's tracks. The crunch of the tires on the ground was instantly gone. Julie listened for her bike and heard nothing, only the sound of her own breathing. Why didn't she hear any birds or wind or anything? It felt as if the trees were holding their breath.

Shivering, she looked up at the armlike branches. The trees seemed to be leaning in toward her. Knots in the bark looked almost like faces. Shadows leered at her. She thought she saw something out of the corner of her eye and turned quickly, but nothing moved.

"Safe inside the Wild," she mocked herself. Anything and everything—witches, wolves, goblins, trolls—could be hiding in the misshapen shadows. This was the Wild Wood. This was the place where Mom had lived and Dad had died.

Deep breath, she told herself. Don't panic. She had a plan: she'd follow the streets (or what was left of them) through downtown to the Wishing Well Motel—the last place that Cindy and Goldie had seen Mom. With luck, Mom would still be there. Of course, if Julie hadn't lost the boots, she could have been there and back already. Now she'd have to do it on foot. But the plan still held, right?

Tromping over bushes and ferns, she headed back toward the path. She'd left it to chase the bike. Stupid, stupid, stupid, she thought. She hadn't been in the Wild for a full minute before she'd lost the boots, the bike, and the path.

It hit her like a slap: she'd lost the path.

She'd run straight. It should be right here. She should have found it by now. Julie scanned the forest: dark, crooked trees . . . all the same.

No, no, no! She couldn't be lost. How could she be lost? She hadn't run far. The street had to be near. She'd just picked the wrong direction. It must be over there . . . Backtracking, she tried another direction.

No path.

Gillian was out there playing the trumpet for wild animals so that Julie could come here, and Julie was lost after two minutes. She'd wasted Gillian's bravery.

Mom would be so disappointed.

Balling her hands into fists, Julie swallowed hard again and again. Don't cry, she told herself. Don't cry, don't cry. She just had to stay calm and not panic and it would all be okay. She couldn't be far from the former West Street.

It wasn't as if the Wild could rearrange geography. (Could it?) She'd seen that gas station—the Wild didn't transform everything. It wasn't all-powerful. (Was it?)

"I'm trying, Mom," she said aloud. "Doesn't that count?" How could it count? If she didn't succeed, Mom would never know she'd tried.

Then I'll just have to succeed, she thought. She might have lost her bike and the Seven League Boots, but she still had all the magic supplies from the linen closet. She wasn't helpless. She could do this. Straightening her shoulders, she picked a different direction and began to walk.

As she went deeper into the forest, the woods thickened. Ancient-looking ferns and thorny bushes filled the gaps between the trees, creating a lacework of menacing shadows. She climbed over fallen logs and massive roots.

How like a fairy tale, she thought, a girl lost in the woods. She tried not to think about the things that happened to little girls lost in woods. Maybe she was more like the simpleton heroes, wandering lost until they met the creatures that would make their fortunes—she wasn't sure if that was better or worse.

I hate this, she thought. I really hate this.

She climbed over another root and spotted, up ahead, what looked like a string of Christmas lights between the ferns. Maybe it was a house. If it was a house, then a street had to be nearby! She picked up her pace.

Drawing closer, she saw the lights weren't decorations; they were flowers—beautiful, unnaturally bright flowers that glowed with their own brilliance. She heard humming—someone was there. Julie froze, listening. It was a woman's voice, and the tune was a cross between "Twinkle, Twinkle" and "Row, Row, Row Your Boat." Julie wiped her sweaty palms on her jeans and crept forward. In between the trees, she saw a girl in a red cape and hood picking flowers. Little Red? How could it be? Ms. Hood was in France.

The girl turned her head as she picked a brilliant red daisy, and Julie's eyes widened. Oh, wow. It wasn't the Little Red she knew. It was someone else, someone older. Under the red cape, a forty-year-old woman wore a business suit. Staring, Julie forgot to hide.

"Look at my beautiful flowers," the false Little Red said, smiling brightly. "I'm picking them for Grandma." Julie opened her mouth, but no words came out. The woman hopped over a root and pounced on a shimmering purple flower. "Grandma loves flowers," she said.

This was what Julie's grandmother had told her about, the danger of the Wild. Somehow, this businesswoman had become a new Little Red. Julie managed to get her voice to work: "I'm, ah, looking for the path."

"I've strayed from the path," New Little Red said. "I'm picking flowers." She spun the bouquet in her hands. It was almost hypnotic, a sort of kaleidoscope. Julie tore her eyes from it. All her instincts told her to run away—far, far away. "Do you know where the path is?" Julie asked.

"It's over there," New Little Red said, gesturing nonchalantly over her shoulder. "Mother said not to leave it."

Yes! Julie peered through the trees, but she didn't see anything. Maybe it was on the other side of the trees. Julie began to wade through bushes.

Behind her, the businesswoman giggled over a patch of yellow flowers that glowed like mini-suns. It was a horribly vacant sound. Julie hesitated. She couldn't just leave her like this. Something was obviously wrong with her, and she could be walking right into the jaws of danger. Literally. "You didn't happen to meet a wolf, did you?" Julie asked.

"He was a very nice wolf," New Little Red said.

She had guessed right: this woman had set off a fairy-tale event, just like Grandma said would happen. She was caught in one of the Wild's puppet plays. But that didn't explain the weird blankness. Shouldn't she at least know who she was, even if she couldn't help what she did? "You shouldn't be picking flowers. The wolf is on his way to your grandmother's house."

"Do you think Grandma would like the blue ones?" New Little Red said.

Julie tried again. "You're not Little Red Riding Hood. You have to snap out of it. You're in a fairy tale. A wolf is going to eat you."

"Grandma will like these flowers," the woman said. She smiled vapidly at Julie.

Goose bumps ran up and down Julie's arms. It was okay if she ran, Julie rationalized. The woman was a grown-up. She could take care of herself. But the wolf . . . "Look, I can tell you what will happen: the wolf will be in your grandmother's clothes. You'll do the whole 'Grandma, how big your eyes are' thing, and you'll get to 'Grandma, how big your teeth are' and he'll eat you," Julie said. "You can't go to your grandmother's house."

New Little Red's eyes narrowed. "I *am* going to Grandma's house."

What was Julie supposed to do? She couldn't force the woman not to go. Maybe she could try to take the flowers away. Julie reached for the stems.

"No! Grandma's flowers!" New Little Red swatted Julie with the petals. Julie jumped backward, and New Little Red advanced on her. "Bad girl! *Bad* girl!" The forty-year-old woman, face terrible in anger, shook the flowers at Julie.

"But . . ." Julie said.

The woman's eyes widened. "You have my picnic basket!" she shrieked. She pointed at Julie's backpack. "My basket for Grandma!"

Before Julie could react, New Little Red launched at her and seized the backpack. She ripped it off Julie. Julie clung to the shoulder straps. "No! It's mine! I need it! Please!" Julie begged.

"My basket!" the woman yelled. "My basket for Grandma!" She tugged on it, and Julie stumbled forward. The woman was stronger than she was. But she couldn't let her take the backpack. It held all of her magic. She needed it. How would she make it through the woods without it?

"Please! My mother . . ."

"Wolf! Wolf, she's taking the basket! The basket for Grandma!" New Little Red shouted. "Wolf!"

Julie heard branches break. And she heard a growl—a deep, horrible, hair-raising growl that she felt inside her stomach. Oh, no! The wolf! She let go of the backpack and ran.

Chapter Eleven
Main Street

Julie broke through the bushes and stumbled. She pitched forward and crashed down on her hands and knees. Tears popped into her eyes. *Ow.* She listened for the wolf behind her, and she heard nothing.

He hadn't chased her.

Good.

She'd lost her supplies.

Bad.

She stood and dusted her scraped hands on her jeans. How had she lost her bike, her boots, and her backpack all so quickly? It was like the forest was out to get her. What was it going to take from her next?

She scrutinized the surrounding trees. She was in a broad, flat section of forest. At first, she didn't realize what that meant, and then she saw bits of the real world not quite transformed by the Wild. Telephone poles were fir trees, but their transformers peeked from between fresh leaves, and their wires, wreathed in vines, still linked them together. Lawns were sloped mats of moss. She could see hints of houses, wrapped in green. She'd been right: the Wild didn't transform everything. She'd found a street.

I should be ecstatic, she thought. But she'd lost everything. She was helpless now. And, again, alone. She wished Gillian were here with her. She could use some of her enthusiasm.

Had Mrs. Thomas found Gillian in time? Or was Gillian in the Wild? Was she still playing her trumpet? What was going to happen when she stopped? Would the animals let her stop?

"Psst!"

She jumped.

"No, girl, get down!"

She obeyed and crouched behind a mailbox embedded in a stump.

Just in time. Shrieking and laughing, a train of people ran down the forested street. A boy was stuck to a goose, a girl was stuck to his arm, a man was stuck to her shoulder, and a woman was stuck to his knee. Julie held her breath as the strange bit of story ran past. Somehow it seemed all the more horrible because they—like New Little Red— weren't Mom's friends. These were ordinary people, glued to a goose. She shivered. How did it happen? And how did

Julie keep it from happening to her? The train of people ran between the trees and out of sight. "Too many civilians," another voice said behind her.

Her heart leapt into her throat. "Who's there?" she asked.

"Massachusetts National Guard," came the whispered answer. "You shouldn't be here, miss. The situation is not under control."

Peering into the bushes, she caught a glimpse of them: army men. Heroes! On hands and knees, she crawled closer to them. "Am I glad to see you!" she said.

"We're in hostile territory, miss," the closest man said.

"Tell me about it," Julie said. "Some woman's going to be eaten by a wolf."

The men exchanged glances. "Where?"

She hesitated. Would they believe her if she said Grandma's house? "I mean, it's possible that someone would in a forest like this. Do you know where we are?"

"Crawford Street, approaching Main."

"Oh," she said. She had made zero forward progress. But on the plus side, she wasn't stuck to a goose or picking flowers—at least not yet. And maybe not ever, now that she had found the National Guard. She looked at the hidden soldiers with a growing realization: here was her answer to how she could avoid Little Red's fate. They could help her! She was saved! "I'm searching for my mom," she said. "I think she's—"

"I'll assign someone to take you out of here, miss," the army man said. "Don't you worry. Everything's going to be all right. We'll take care of you."

"No, you don't understand. It will be all right if I can just find my mom," she said, but the soldier was focused on the forest-street. He wasn't listening to her. She tried to get his attention: "Sir? Um, sir?"

"Sir, another one's approaching," a soldier said.

"A victim?" he asked.

"Can't tell, sir."

Julie crawled forward to peer through the bushes, but the captain pulled her back. "You stay here, miss. We'll investigate this." He nodded to two men.

All eleven left the bushes.

"Wait . . ." Julie said. They shouldn't all leave. What if it was a trap, a story bit waiting to entangle them, like New Little Red's wolf? She crawled forward. She could see a woman standing on the street. The woman wore a business suit, a royal cape, and a crown. She held eleven white shirts.

Eleven white shirts. Julie knew this tale. How did it go?

Like moths pulled to flame, the men ran toward the queen. She threw shirts at them. One by one, they turned into swans.

Oh, yes, that was how it went. She felt sick. "Mommy," she whispered. "Where are you?"

* * *

Julie had no choice but to keep going. "I hate this," she said to the trees. The trees were silent—no wind, no birds, no nothing. She had an urge to throw something or shout as loudly as she could—anything to break the awful, waiting silence.

She crept down the forested street, listening for any sounds of people or bits of story. She guessed it was maybe seven miles from here to the Wishing Well Motel. How was she going to avoid being caught in a story for seven miles?

The air began to smell sickly sweet, like cough syrup. She saw roses on the bushes. Up ahead, seven-foot stalks of purple flowers leaned against birches. Fat chrysanthemums engulfed the trunks of evergreens. She guessed this used to be Bigclow Nurseries. Now it had spread to cover the entire street.

This can't be good, Julie thought. Could she go around it? She looked for a way to pass and saw a stream. Bubbling over in miniature rapids, the stream carved a path through the overgrown flowers. She could walk along it. Heading for it, Julie crawled under a low-hanging flowered branch, and the limbs above her erupted in shaking squawks. She covered her head as scattered petals fell down on her.

"Help me!" a voice chirped above her. "Oh, please, kind child, help me!"

Who said that? She looked up and saw a blackbird thrashing against the branches. A tangle of leaves pinned it to its perch.

"Please, set me free!"

Oh, no, Julie thought. When creatures asked for help in fairy tales . . . She began to back away. Her sandal sank into the muddy bank of the stream, and another voice cried out: "Down here! Please, kind child, help me!"

She looked down and saw a fish, stranded. Flopping on the bank, the fish seemed too large to have ever swum in a stream this size. "Save me, please!" The fish flopped pathetically.

Julie felt a sick, fluttery feeling in the pit of her stomach. Had a story found her? What should she do? Should she run? *Could* she run, or was she already trapped? Julie took a tentative step away and a third voice, tiny and shrill, piped up: "Please, spare us!"

Ants. She saw them swarming over the mossy ground. She had nearly squashed them. A chorus of tiny voices, the ants shouted: "If you spare us, we will aid you later!" She knew that phrase: it was a phrase straight out of Grimm's.

She had stumbled onto the animal helpers.

For an instant, she couldn't breathe. In the stories, the hero met the animal helpers before he had to face a villain. Was she going to meet a villain? I don't want to meet a villain, she thought. I want to go home!

All the creatures—bird, fish, and ants—clamored for her: "Save us! Save us!"

She took an involuntary step backward and the ants cried out, "Oh, thank you! Thank you! Someday, we will return to repay your kindness!" The ants scattered across the moss and vanished under a mat of fallen leaves.

Oh, no. She'd done it: a fairy-tale event. She hadn't meant to. She wanted to run. She didn't want to meet an ogre or a witch or a dragon or an evil fairy or a . . .

"Please, save me!" the fish cried.

I can't run, she realized. Refusing to help was just as much a fairy-tale act as helping—except characters who didn't help were always doomed. If a story had found her, she was going to need these creatures to survive whoever or whatever she met next. The tales were very clear about that.

She picked up the fish by its tail fin. Eww, slimy. She dropped it in the water and wiped her hand on her jeans. "Thank you!" it cried. "Someday, I will return to repay your kindness!" She was sure it would—that was the problem. She didn't want to need its help.

In the bush, the bird squawked again. Halfheartedly, Julie tugged at a branch. Snarled, it held fast. She braced herself and yanked. Leaves rustled, the wood bit into her palms, and the bird squirmed free.

"Thank you!" it cried. Julie muttered with it: "Someday,

I will return to repay your kindness." The bird flew up toward the treetops.

Maybe if she got out of the area quickly, she could avoid the villain. Mud sucked at her flip-flops as she hurried down the stream. Maybe this fairy-tale event was an isolated incident. After all, she didn't feel compelled to do anything right now. Maybe she could meet the animal helpers and not have to meet a . . .

Julie heard a crunch, and a pale, slim tree stepped onto the path in front of her. She was 99 percent sure it hadn't been there a second ago.

And she was 99 percent sure it wasn't an ordinary tree. Its bark looked more like scales. Its roots had toenails. Splashing into the stream, she backed away from the "tree." There was a second "tree" beside it with the same scaly bark. She looked up.

Perched on top of enormous chicken legs was the witch's house.

Chapter Twelve
The Witch

Run, Julie thought, staring up at the former Agway rooster sign.

But what if it chased her? She imagined it leaning down to peck, and she shuddered. Maybe she could sneak away. Had the house's owner seen her yet?

Tumbling from the porch, a rope ladder smacked down in front of Julie.

Okay, that would be a "yes." She squinted up at the porch. A face poked over the edge—Julie saw a mass of white, frizzed hair—and then the face disappeared.

It almost looked like . . . No, it couldn't be. Out of the whole forest, Julie couldn't have found her own grandmother so quickly. Could she have? No, it was wishful thinking. Trying to see better, Julie stepped back from the house. The chicken legs stepped forward. Gulping, Julie gawked at the giant legs. Imagining them move was one thing; seeing them move was another.

She heard footsteps on the porch. "Come on up, dearie!" she heard. Julie's heart skipped a beat. That voice! It was Grandma's voice! Wasn't it?

"Grandma, is that you?" she called.

Oh, please, please, let it be her.

Grandma—if it was her—didn't answer. Julie steadied the rope ladder. "Grandma, I'm coming up!" She climbed onto the ladder, and it swayed under her weight, reminding her unpleasantly of the rope climb in gym class. I'm not afraid of heights, she told herself. Just a wee bit terrified of falling. But she could do it if it meant finding Grandma. Slowly, she climbed up the rungs.

One, two, three . . . don't look down . . . nine, ten, eleven . . . At the top, Julie swung her leg up and flopped onto the porch like a beached fish. "Oof."

Knees shaking, she got to her feet.

"Well, now, what a fine, plump girl you are. I think I'll have you basted with a dash of oregano and a sprig of rosemary. And perhaps a squeeze of lemon."

Julie didn't hear her. Her own mind was shouting too loudly: it *was* Grandma! She was alive! She wore a billowy black dress rather than her usual sweats, and her hair was frizzed like a thundercloud, but it was unarguably Gothel. Julie threw her arms around the witch's neck. "Oh, Grandma, I've done everything wrong! I lost the Seven League Boots! And then I helped the ants and the bird and the fish . . ."

The witch squirmed. "Release me, child." She peeled Julie's arms away.

Gulping down a sob, Julie let go. "Grandma?" Wasn't she glad to see her? Or was she angry because Julie was in the Wild? Did she think Julie shouldn't have come? Julie was beginning to think she shouldn't have come—she'd probably made the Wild grow with the story bit with the animal helpers. "I'm sorry," Julie said.

"Unprecedented. Inappropriate," the witch muttered. She flattened her hair and straightened her dress. "Let's start over, shall we?" The witch tapped a crooked finger on Julie's arm. "Well, now, what a fine, plump girl you are," she said. "I will have you basted . . ."

Basted? *Plump?* Grandma called her *plump?* "Grandma?"

The witch scowled. "Stop calling me that, child."

For an instant, Julie didn't understand. Didn't Grandma recognize her? Staring at her grandmother in confusion, she noticed Gothel's eyes were their natural color: red. She wasn't wearing her tinted contact lenses, Julie realized with relief. That explained it! She probably couldn't see Julie as more than a blur. (A plump blur, Julie thought.) Julie leaned in so Gothel could see her better. "It's me. Julie. Grandma, don't you recognize me?"

The witch squinted at Julie. "You weren't the one I turned into a flower, were you?"

Stricken, Julie opened and shut her mouth. It wasn't

just the lenses: Gothel didn't know her. Her own grand-mother didn't know her.

"Or, I know," the witch said, "you're the squirrel."

No, no, no! She had to recognize her! "It's me! Your granddaughter! Julie Marchen!" Julie clutched her grand-mother's wide sleeve. "Don't you remember me?"

The witch pried the fabric out of Julie's fingers. "This is not how it is done," she said. She drew herself up to full height, and Julie instinctively shrank back. "You must perform a task for me," the witch said.

Julie felt as if she'd been hit in the stomach. "T-task?" she repeated.

"I have emptied a dish of lentils into the ashes for you. You must separate them out," the witch said. She pointed to a gray pile of dust and a silver bowl. "Succeed, and I shall reward you. Fail, and I shall have you for my dinner." And then the witch took her broomstick and leapt off the lip of the porch.

* * *

Dazed, Julie sank down on the porch. What had just happened? Did her own grandmother really just threaten to *eat* her? Why didn't Grandma remember her?

Julie thought of the New Little Red, blithely picking flowers. Grandma had acted like that, consumed by the fairy tale. Was it because she was in a fairy tale?

But that didn't make sense. Julie was involved in a fairy-tale sequence now too, but she still had all her memories. She knew who she was. Why did Grandma have this weird amnesia but not Julie? What did the Wild do to her?

Maybe the Little Red woman had just cracked under the strain, but Grandma was one of the strongest personalities Julie knew. Julie had an awful thought: if the Wild had done this to Grandma, what had it done to Mom?

She had to get out of here. She had to find Mom. Julie jumped to her feet and hurried to the ladder . . .

It wasn't there. Dropping to her stomach, she looked over the lip of the porch. No ladder. The witch must have taken it. How was Julie going to get down?

She studied the surrounding trees. She'd never climbed a tree so tall in her life. She reached out to touch a branch. The chicken legs took a step backward, and the leaves slipped out of her fingers. She was trapped. What was she going to do?

A blackbird cleared its throat. "Ahem?"

She looked up. The bird she'd freed! The first animal helper! She was saved! "Can you help me get down?"

He ruffled his feathers, confused. "No. But you have lentils in the ashes."

For an instant, she had no idea what he was talking about, and then she remembered the witch's task. "Oh. Right." She shouldn't have been surprised: he was an ani-

mal helper, and here was his task. "Please, be my guest."
Leaning back his head, the bird caroled. Leaves shook as
fluttering sounds filled the woods, and birds burst out of
the branches and swooped onto the porch. A mass of
feathers, the birds pecked at the pile of ashes. Lentil after
lentil hit the dish with tiny pings.

As suddenly as they had come, the birds swarmed into
the air and vanished in a flurry of wings. "Uh, thanks," she
said to the empty air. She didn't know whether to feel
grateful or unnerved. She picked up the lentils as the
witch swooped onto the porch.

"Basted or broiled?" the witch said.

"Grandma . . ." Her throat clogged. Oh, Grandma!
Seeing her like this . . . it was wrong. Yes, Julie knew the
stories, but they were Grandma's past. She'd left this
behind centuries ago. She wasn't evil anymore. She was
Julie's grandmother—fun and smart and sweet and wild.

Julie held out the dish, and the witch reached for it.
Instinctively, Julie gripped the bowl. "Can you hear me,
Grandma?" She searched the witch's red eyes.
Somewhere deep inside the witch was Grandma. She had
to be. Julie refused to believe she was gone. "I know
you're in there. Grandma, it's me, Julie. Rapunzel's
daughter. Remember Zel?"

Gothel's face contorted, and Julie held her breath—did
she remember?—then the expression vanished. Julie's heart

sank. The witch yanked the dish out of her hands and threw it against the wall of the house. Lentils spilled over the floor.

"There are a thousand pearls hidden on the forest floor," the witch said. "You must gather them for me." Grabbing hold of Julie, the witch pulled her onto the broom. Julie yelped as the broom zoomed out of the doorway and then burst up through the branches of the trees.

Julie and the witch skimmed low over the leaves. Gripping the broom, Julie tucked her feet up as branches slapped her ankles. "Ow, ow, ow!" Without warning, the witch pointed the nose of the broom down, and they dove straight between the trees. Shrieking, Julie shut her eyes as the ground raced up at them. Inches from impact, the witch pulled the broom straight and they zipped over the ground. Dodging trees trunks, they flew along the forest floor.

The witch pulled to a stop, and Julie slid over the front of the broom. She clung to the tip, and the witch rapped Julie's fingers with knobbed knuckles. Julie released the broom. A foot from the ground, she landed hard.

Cackling, the witch flew off into the forest. Slowly, Julie's heart rate returned to normal and her stomach settled down from her throat. She looked at the surrounding forest, silent and waiting. I could run, she thought. Grandma was gone, and she was out of the chicken house. She could escape this fairy tale and go back to searching for Mom.

Or go get caught in a different story.

If only she could've made Grandma remember, then Grandma could've rescued Mom and they'd all be home by now.

Julie heard a soft clink at her feet, and she looked down. The ants were piling pearls into a mini-pyramid. She'd get another chance, she realized. She could try again. The witch would return when the ants were done.

Should she stay? Grandma had almost remembered. Julie was sure of it. If she'd just had a little more time, she would have broken through.

She had to try.

Julie looked up at the sky, waiting for Grandma to reappear as the ants completed the second impossible task.

* * *

The witch cackled as she landed beside Julie. "Do you have my pearls?"

Julie scooped up the pearls and carried them to her grandmother. She poured them into the witch's waiting hands. "You're Dame Gothel Marchen," she said as she poured. "You own the Wishing Well Motel. You guard the wishing well. Someone made a wish for the Wild to be free, and you were trapped . . ."

The witch frowned at her. "Motel . . ." For an instant, Julie thought: It's working! It's working! But then the witch shook herself. "No nonsense from you," she said. "As I flew across the forest, a ring fell off my finger and landed in one of the streams. You will find it for me."

Was it her imagination, or did the witch sound less certain? Was Julie reaching her? In a swirl of cape, the witch leapt onto her broom and flew up into the treetops. Leaves rained down on Julie below.

She'd have one more chance, she told herself, once she found the ring.

The ring was in a stream, the witch had said. Julie listened for running water. She walked toward the sound and found a fish waiting patiently for her. He poked his mouth out of the water. "How can I be of aid?" he asked.

She wasn't surprised to see him. He was the third animal helper; this was his task. The Wild pulled no punches when arranging coincidences. Was this how it trapped people? By making its stories inevitable? "I need the ring that the witch dropped into one of the streams a few minutes ago. Can you find it for me?"

"Consider it done," the fish said. With a regal bow (for a fish), he ducked back under the water. Soon, she saw schools of fish swimming toward him. He swam against the tide, and she heard the burble of fish voices as he asked the other fish about the ring. Fish after fish shook their fish heads, until the water wuffled above them.

Julie saw a tiny streak of silver—a guppy racing

through the water. "Wait! I'm here! I'm here!" the guppy cried. Gulping, she braked with her tail fin. In a formal voice, as if reciting lines, she said, "Please accept my apology. I would not have been late, except as I was swimming, a ring fell out of the heavens and struck me."

"You have done well," Julie's fish said. "Can you lead us to the ring?"

Julie followed onshore as the school of fish stretched into a long parade. As the stream became shallower, some of the fish had to leap over rocks to avoid stranding themselves. The forest filled with the sound of breaching fish.

Finally, the guppy halted. Julie bent over the stream. Wedged between stones, the ring sparkled in a shaft of sunlight. She reached into the cold water and picked it up. A band of carved leaves of pink and yellow gold, the ring winked in the sun as she turned it over in her hand. She felt a lump in her throat. She knew this ring: her mother had given it to Gothel for her birthday two years ago. If Julie couldn't make Grandma remember this time . . .

Cackling, the witch soared overhead, and the fish scattered, swimming up and downstream as fast as their fins would take them. The witch landed.

Julie held out the ring. Snarling, the witch reached for it, but Julie snatched it away. "Do you remember this ring?" Julie asked, waving it at her. "It was dwarf-made. My mother gave it to you. We had chocolate cake, and it was covered in so many candles that we melted the frosting." Remembering, she wanted to cry. Julie saw the witch's gnarled hands were shaking. "You can do it, Grandma," Julie said. "Fight the Wild. You used to babysit me. Remember? You used to make shadow puppets on the wall, entire scenes of shadows with your hands. You used to let me stir your cauldrons. We gathered newts together. Remember. You gave me a talking frog for my fifth birthday, and I brought it in to show-and-tell, and Mom made you change it back into the mailman. Please, remember. Where's my mother?"

"Julie?" Gothel said.

Chapter Thirteen
Reminders

Gothel bear-hugged Julie. "Oh, Julie, Julie, my little Julie." Julie hugged her back just as hard. Grandma remembered! She was free! Bony fingers dug into Julie's shoulders, and Gothel pushed her to arm's length. "You shouldn't be here," Gothel said fiercely.

Julie couldn't have agreed more. "I'm sorry!"

Gothel relaxed her hold on Julie's shoulders. "Suppose I should have expected it, given who your mother is." She smiled at Julie. "She used to be the one to bring me back to myself." Hobbling nearer to the stream, Gothel eased herself down onto one of the boulders. Julie nearly shrieked—what was she doing? They didn't have time for sitting. They had to rescue Mom! Gothel continued, "She was the one who found the trick of it, you know: leaving reminders for herself, jump-starting all our memories every time each of us forgot."

What was she talking about? "Grandma, we can't stay here." She tugged on her hand. "We have to find Mom and get out of here. The Wild's practically across Northboro already."

Gothel stayed seated on the rock. "You are so like your mother," she said.

She wasn't at all like Mom. Julie didn't understand half of the things Mom said and did. Like having the dwarves over for dinner. Or caring about her stupid hair salon. Or not understanding why Julie was miserable at school and miserable at home. Or worst of all: leaving Julie alone while the Wild took over the world. Julie wiped her nose with the back of her hand. Her cheeks felt stiff, and she had a sour taste in her mouth. "Grandma . . . I wished she wasn't my mother."

"Zel knew you didn't mean it," Gothel said.

She thought of the look on Mom's face and knew that Grandma was just saying that to make her feel better. She took a deep breath. "I did mean it," she said. "When I said it, I meant it. But I didn't mean . . . for this . . ." She waved her arm at the thick trees, blocking the sky.

"That's the beauty of the real world," Gothel said. "Wishing doesn't make it so. Outside the Wild, it's actions that matter. Your choices matter." Her grandmother reached over and squeezed her hand. "This isn't your fault. Your wish didn't make any of this happen."

Cindy had said the same thing—it wasn't possible that her wish had caused this. It wasn't a magic wish. Julie already knew that. But what if Mom thought that Julie wanted her back in the Wild? What if Mom believed that Julie truly wanted her gone? "Grandma, where's Mom?"

"Right where I put her," Gothel said.

"Really?" Julie said, feeling a smile spread over her face. Grandma had kept Mom safe! It was going to be over soon. It was all okay.

"I'm afraid so," Gothel said. "She's in her tower."

Or not "all okay." Julie let go of her grandmother's hand as if it had stung her.

Gothel sighed. "It's a new tower. She'll have to make new reminders. She'll have to be clever with them—the Wild knows all her old tricks."

"Reminders?" Julie asked.

"The Wild doesn't transform everything every time; it only changes what's necessary for the story to happen. So Zel used to leave clues for herself to trigger her memories. She called them her 'reminders.' Sometimes she wrote letters to herself on the walls of her tower, different stones each time. Sometimes she left clues in her embroidery. Sometimes she shaped hints out of strands of her hair. Near the end, she wrote messages with her own blood."

Mom did that? Wrote in her own blood? Julie couldn't imagine her dainty mother doing anything like that. "Why?"

"When you end a story, the Wild locks you down deep inside yourself and forces you to reenact the first event of that story. That beginning is all you know, until and unless someone or something makes you remember," she said. "That's how it traps you." She smiled wanly at Julie. "You are fortunate that this isn't a sequence at the end of a story. If it were an ending, you too would have lost your memory and you'd now be the poor stepdaughter sent into the woods on your stepmother's whim. You wouldn't remember ever being anything different."

If that was true (and she believed everything except Mom and the blood), there was no time to waste. Had Mom ended a story? When Grandma rescued her, would Mom remember Julie? Julie wasn't sure she could stand it if Mom didn't know her. Julie took Grandma's hand. "But now you do remember, and we can go find Mom."

Gothel extracted her hand from Julie's. "It's not that simple."

But . . . but she remembered! Now she could come with Julie, rescue Mom, shrink the Wild, and leave. There was nothing stopping her now. "Why not?"

Her red eyes sad, Grandma said, "Oh, Julie. I can't be free. No matter how I believed I'd changed, no matter how many years passed . . . I'm the witch. The Wild knew my role as soon as I entered—it owns me. Even if I were to try to escape in between events, the Wild would simply find another story bit that suited me. There are a dozen different tales that could trap me."

Julie felt her hopes crumble. "But . . . But . . ." She had an idea, and she grabbed it as if she were drowning: "But what about my reward? This story bit says I get a reward. I want you to . . ." Julie began. The witch waved her hand. ". . . rescue Mom," Julie finished. A rose and a diamond fell from her mouth. "Ow!" A sapphire popped onto her tongue. She spit it out. "It hurts!" she wailed. "Make it stop!" Her gums bled from the thorns as roses tumbled over her lips.

Gothel waved her other hand.

"That was terrible," Julie said. No jewels or flowers fell out. She wiped the blood from her mouth on her sleeve. "Why did you do that?"

"It is what I do," Grandma said sadly. "All the years outside the Wild, all the years of not playing the villain . . . yet here I am again, and this is what I am. Maybe it's what I've always been." Overhead, the wind blew through the leaves, as if agreeing with Gothel. Maybe it was.

"You're not a villain. You shouldn't listen to stupid, evil trees." She spat bloody saliva at the foot of the nearest tree. "Can I have my mother for my reward?"

"I can't do that," Gothel said. "I don't have that power. Only a wishing ring can take you to her."

Julie thought of all the items in her backpack. Had one of them been a wishing ring? If only she hadn't lost it! "Can you give me one?" Julie asked.

Gothel shook her head. "There's only one. The magician keeps it on a chain around his neck while he's awake and in his mouth while he's asleep."

"Can you take me to the magician?" she asked.

"Only the ogre can take you there."

Julie rolled her eyes. "Okay. Can you take me to the ogre?"

"You must cross the endless ocean."

Of course the Wild wouldn't make it easy for her. Witches, ogres, magicians . . . Julie felt her stomach flip-flop. She wasn't getting out of a story; she was getting deeper *in*. "Can you help at all?"

Gothel's face contorted, as if she were fighting with herself. "I am sorry," she said. "You must go. It's not safe for you to be near me. Go while you can. Go before the Wild finds a role that suits you."

She couldn't leave her. She couldn't go on alone. "Grandma, please!"

"Stay clear of stories. Especially endings." Grandma hugged her quickly, and Julie tried to cling to her. Grandma pushed her to arm's length.

Julie felt like crying. "Grandma . . ."

"Run. *Please*." There was something in her voice. Something strange. Something scary. Julie turned from her grandmother and ran.

Chapter Fourteen
Wild Bikes

Sheer crystal, the glass mountain flashed in the sun. Rainbows danced over the grass and trees. Etched in the slope in front of her, Julie read the former sign: WARD HILL SKI AND RECREATION CENTER. With a sinking heart, she blinked up at the sparkling crystal ski slope. The Wild had grown. She was a full mile beyond where she'd left Gillian.

Unless Mrs. Thomas and Rachel had reached her in time, Julie was certain Gillian was in the Wild. Somewhere. Julie shouldn't have let her get so close. Never mind that Gillian had wanted to come—Julie had known better. And now the Wild most likely had Gillian and was making her live out a story. Please let it be a safe story. Please let her be okay.

She'll be okay, Julie thought, just as soon as I find Mom and Mom stops the Wild—which would happen as soon as she found the endless sea and the ogre and the magician . . . "We're doomed," Julie said.

As if cued by her words, leaves crackled. Branches snapped. Something fast, furry, and orange darted past her. Julie flattened against a tree as a pack of riderless bicycles raced in pursuit. Near the center of the pack, her own ten-speed bounced over the rocks and roots. Her boots, still tied to the handlebars, flapped against the frame.

Her bike! Her boots! She needed those! "Wait! Bike!"

Up ahead, their prey squealed.

Her bike was hunting. How dare it! "Hey!" Julie yelled. "Bike, get back here!" She chased after it, following the path of flattened bushes and ferns.

In a clearing, the bikes circled. She saw a huddled shape through the blur of bike wheels. Front wheels feinted toward the creature, and the animal shrieked. They were going to hurt it. Maybe kill it. She couldn't let her own bike do that! Without stopping to think, she bent down, picked up a stick, and threw it at the tires. "Stop it!" she shouted. "Leave it alone!" She threw more sticks and rocks, anything that her hand grabbed.

The bikes broke out of their circle. Oh, no. Her heart thumped faster. Now the bikes would chase her. They'd run her down. Julie backed against a tree.

But the bikes simply dispersed into the forest. Julie

released a breath she hadn't known she'd been holding. That was close.

Cautiously, she came out of the trees. In the center of the clearing, the lump of cloth whimpered. "Are you okay?" Julie asked, bending down.

The cloth was familiar: it was Boots's cloak. Could it be . . . She pulled back the cloth. An orange tiger-striped cat huddled in a ball. It was Boots! Wait—what if he was lost in a story? What if talking to him would trap her in another fairy-tale event?

He raised his head. "Julie?"

He knew her! She leaned forward to hug him and then stopped again. Just because he knew her didn't mean he wasn't in a story. It only meant that he hadn't reached an ending yet. Grandma had said that only story endings caused memory loss. Boots could still be part of a story that could trap her. "Are you okay?"

Sitting upright, he began to lick himself. "I lost a bit of tail fur to a talking hedge that I ran through. Everything here seems to have cat on its dinner menu. I think I created several new stories—all of them full of chase scenes. Sheer luck that none of the scenes were endings. If things in here weren't so jumbled, I would have been doomed." He shuddered and said, "I'd forgotten how horrible this place is. Can we please go home now?"

He wanted to go home! "Home" was still with her!

Julie scooped him into her arms and hugged him. "I'm sorry I said you were a rat," she said into his fur. "You are a rotten brother sometimes, but you aren't a rat."

He squirmed. "Hey," he said, "enough with the mushy stuff. Good to see you too. Thanks for saving my life and all that. Can we leave now? Please? Before my luck runs out? I admit I was wrong, okay? I haven't found the love of my life; I've only found trouble."

She put him down, feeling better than she had since she'd come into the woods. She had her brother back. "Mom will get us out of here," Julie said. She felt more sure than ever.

"She's here?" Boots peered into the trees. "She did it again?"

"Again?" Julie asked.

He trotted toward the shrubbery. "When we first escaped, she was the one who came to us, woke our memories, and gathered us together. She was amazing. Like a general." Standing up in his boots, he poked his nose between the ferns. "Rapunzel?"

Like a general? She stared at him.

"Rapunzel!"

"She's not here. An ogre has to take me to a magician who has a ring that can take me to her," Julie said. "What do you mean, she was the one who gathered you?"

The cat blinked at her. "Is that the direct route?"

"After I cross the endless ocean," she admitted. "I don't suppose you know how to cross an endless ocean?"

"Course I know how to cross it," Boots said. "I'm old buddies with the griffin." He trotted decisively through the trees.

She followed after him. "Griffin?" she asked.

"How else would you get across the ocean?"

"Boat?" she suggested.

"Don't be ridiculous."

Chapter Fifteen
The Griffin

On the Route 290 bridge over Lake Quinsigamond, the griffin sunned himself. He stretched, exposing his lion stomach, across three lanes. Shortly beyond him, the bridge ended in midair. Blueness stretched on and on into the horizon.

Julie tried to sound casual. "You know, Worcester used to be on the other side of this bridge." Even to her own ears, her voice sounded weak. "I also don't recall a griffin last time I was here."

"Stay clear of his beak," Boots said as he trotted onto the bridge.

She wasn't tempted to go anywhere near his beak. In fact, she didn't want to step onto the bridge. She looked down at her feet. Moss blanketed the ground beneath her mud-crusted flip-flops. Here the earth was comfortably solid. In front of her, the exposed asphalt of the bridge was riddled with tiny cracks like an old oil painting. Worse, it was moving. Untethered at one end, steel supports dangling in the water, the former highway swayed in the wind. Gusts swept the bridge back and forth, like a lashing cat tail, in rhythm with the waves.

Boots was already a third of the way across the bridge. He stopped to wait for her. "Come on, scaredy-cat."

"Look who's talking," Julie said. She stepped off the moss and started toward him. "You're the one who was running from a bicycle."

He ruffled his fur, indignant. "It hunted with a pack!"

"Ooh, look out! Here comes a tricycle!"

Scowling at her, Boots said, "Very funny."

Snoring, the griffin clawed the asphalt. The pavement splintered, and Julie dropped to her knees as a crack ran diagonally across the bridge. The crack hit the median strip, but the median held. Julie's heart thudded. That's it, she thought, I'm going back. Boots sniffed at the crack. Crawling forward, Julie joined him. She could see a strip of blue through the asphalt.

"I hate water," Boots said, jumping across the crack.

You can do it, Julie told herself. It's only water. Standing, she stepped over the crack. Eyes down, she watched the pavement for more incipient cracks as she walked quickly toward the end.

Boots stopped. She raised her head.

She had seen a lot of illustrations in various fairy-tale

books, but none had prepared her for just how big a full-grown griffin was. A griffin on an 8½-by-11-inch page was one thing; a griffin the size of a Greyhound bus was another. His eagle beak was more like a *T. rex* jaw, and his serpent tail resembled an Amazonian anaconda. Feathers blended into pelt blended into scales, all over a mass of predatory muscle. Julie swallowed. "Close enough, don't you think?" she whispered to Boots.

He nodded fervently.

"Should we wake him up?"

A less enthusiastic nod.

Julie wet her lips. How should she do it? What if he woke up cranky? "Um, hello, Mr. Griffin?" Snorting, the griffin flopped his snake tail to the side. Julie and Boots exchanged glances, and Julie tried again: "Good morning. Uh, sorry to bother you."

One yellow eye opened. "Oh, no," the griffin said. "Tourists."

The cat sauntered up to the griffin and leaned a paw against the bulk of his snake tail. "Got a favor to ask, ol' buddy, ol' pal. How would you feel about a little jaunt across the water, ol' buddy, ol' friend?" He punched the griffin on his haunch.

"I can't even begin to tell you how utterly uninterested I am," the griffin said. He twitched his leg, and Boots sprang backward.

"But . . ." the cat sputtered.

"It is considered rude to eat acquaintances, but in your case, I could make an exception." Pointedly, the griffin opened his beak and snapped it shut. Julie jumped. "Take your turn-a-beggar-into-a-queen scheme elsewhere. Do not make me part of your story." He lowered his head and closed his eyes.

Boots darted behind Julie. "Old buddies?" she whispered at him, eyeing the griffin's beak. Slowly, they backed away from the griffin. "I expected his grandfather," the cat whispered to her. "This griffin was born after we escaped the Wild. But don't worry. We'll find another way to cross the ocean."

"There's another way?" she asked.

"Not really, no."

She stopped retreating. "What do you mean, 'no'?"

"C'mon, I saw him eat a cow once. Wasn't pretty."

Julie looked across the water toward the horizon. The waves broke into white crests near the bridge and darkened into deep blue beyond. If Mom were here, what would she do? She would do the sensible thing, Julie answered herself: get off the bridge and away from the griffin.

Wouldn't she? Julie thought about what Grandma had said about Mom leaving "reminders" in blood and what Boots had said about her being the one to gather everyone, and suddenly, Julie wasn't so sure. Would Mom be scared of a griffin?

Julie tried to remember when she'd last seen her mom

scared. Oddly, she couldn't think of a single time. Was that possible? "Was Mom scared last time she was in the Wild?" Julie asked Boots.

"Rapunzel?" he asked, surprised.

The griffin opened one eye.

"Sure," Boots said. "Maybe . . ." He considered it. "I don't know. She was pretty mad." He shot a look at the griffin. "Uh-uh, you aren't planning to . . ." Straightening her shoulders, she walked toward the griffin. "Mr. Griffin . . ." she began.

"You're *her* daughter?" the griffin said.

Julie hesitated. Was that a good thing or a bad thing? She'd thought she had it rough as the daughter of fairy-tale characters, but at least she was human. If a talking cat had had problems in the outside world, it couldn't have been fun for a griffin. He might not want her to find her mother. He might want to stay in the Wild where he could sun on bridges instead of hiding from human sight. "Yes?" she said in a small voice. If he wanted to stop her, he could. The griffin ate cows; she'd be a nice appetizer.

The mass of lion-eagle-serpent uncoiled, and Julie shrank back. Standing, he towered, dinosaur-sized, over them. "Well, why didn't you say so in the first place? I am a great admirer. I have studied her deeds in the Great Battle. We have never had a hero like her."

"Mom's not a hero," Julie said automatically. "She's Rapunzel."

"She rode into battle on the back of my grandfather," the griffin said proudly. "Ah, it must have been glorious."

"Messy, actually," Boots said. "Stories ending left and right. Friends forgetting and turning into enemies right before our eyes. Still have nightmares about it."

Julie realized her mouth was hanging open. She shut it. Her mother was in a battle? She pictured Mom with scissors in one hand and a curl brush in the other riding a griffin. "You're joking."

"It was genius strategy," the griffin said, "a plan that no one but the brilliant Rapunzel could have concocted. And it would have succeeded . . ."

". . . if it weren't for the whole doomed-to-failure part," Boots said.

The griffin glared at him. "It would have succeeded had not the odds been so overwhelming. How does one fight a force of nature? You'd do as well to reject gravity."

Julie felt excitement rising. Could this be true? Could this Great Battle be Mom's secret past? "What happened?"

"We lost," Boots said shortly. "It won."

"Through deceit, the Wild recaptured the valiant rebels," the griffin said.

"Tricked into story endings; forced to reenact beginnings; memories gone," Boots said. "Do we have to talk about this?"

"But someone did stop the Wild," Julie said. "It was defeated."

"Yes, but it was many, many years later," the griffin

said. "Many, many years of repeating the same actions, saying the same words . . ."

"How was it stopped?" she pressed.

The griffin looked uncomfortable. "My grandfather says that none but Rapunzel and her prince know. But all know the glory of her battle!" ("Once they remembered it," Boots interjected.) "Minstrels sing of it! Poets write of it!" The griffin fanned his wings and crowed. Julie clapped her hands over her ears. She lowered them when the griffin settled down again. "She went to battle to break the endless cycles of stories by preventing the endings. She and her army chopped beanstalks before Jacks could climb them, stole glass shoes before princes could find them . . . For a while, there was glorious chaos!"

"And then it ended," Boots interrupted.

The griffin bowed his head. "And then it ended," he intoned.

"Can we get on with this, please?" Boots said. "Are you going to give us a ride or not?"

"Yes, yes, of course," the griffin said. He ruffled his feathers. "You know the rules? Of course, you do. You are Rapunzel's daughter." He lowered his head to the bridge. "Climb on my back and we'll be off."

Julie couldn't picture it: her mother in a battle. Their Rapunzel and her mother felt like two separate people. Their Rapunzel was a stranger. She had to know more. "But my mom—"

Boots interrupted: "The sooner we cross the ocean, the sooner we find Zel. She can tell you all about it then."

He was right. She could ask Mom all her questions. Suddenly, Julie felt even more impatient to find her. Holding on to feathers, Julie climbed onto the griffin.

The griffin raised his head, and Julie and the cat slid down the neck feathers until Julie's thighs hit the griffin's shoulders. "Wish he came with seat belts," Julie said. She held on to two five-foot feathers as the griffin pumped his wings. Half hopping, half running, the griffin headed for the end of the bridge. His wings pumped harder. His paws pushed off beneath him. He leapt off the edge of the bridge.

They fell toward the roiling waters, and Julie's stomach lurched; then his wings caught wind, and they were lifted up.

*   *   *

She felt as if she could fly forever. Beautiful blue water sparkled below her. Cool wind streamed in her face. She laughed out loud. "This is amazing!" she shouted into the wind. "Boots, isn't this amazing?"

Shivering, Boots huddled in front of her.

Julie stretched her arms out to either side. She was soaring. Voice rumbling underneath her, the griffin said, "We are almost halfway across. Soon, I must rest."

Julie peeked over the griffin's neck. Water swelled and crested in windborne waves. Rest? "But there's no land!"

"If you have a walnut, you must drop it now and it will

grow into a tree on which I can rest. Otherwise, I must throw you into the sea or I will not make it to the other side."

"What!" Julie shrieked. "But I don't have a walnut! I don't have any magic things. I lost them all!"

Boots yelped. "I hate water!"

"You can't drop us!" Julie said. "Please! We'll drown!"

"It's not my choice," the griffin said irritably. "It's the rules. I asked you if you knew them. If you cross the ocean on the griffin's back, this is how this story bit goes. I am sorry, especially considering your mother, but any second now, I will shake you off my back. If it's any consolation, it's the Wild that will do it, not me."

He couldn't be serious. "Some consolation . . ." Julie began.

The griffin dove toward the water. Julie shrieked and clutched his feathers as he tilted sideways. His feathers grazed the waves, and then he flipped upside down. Julie and the cat dangled.

Upside down, the griffin shook his back. Feathers slipped through Julie's fingers. Boots yowled as he lost his grip. "Boots! No!" Julie yelled. He splashed into the sea. Sputtering, he bobbed between the waves. Boots!

Without stopping to think, Julie released the griffin's feathers. Screaming, she flailed at the air. She splashed into the water.

Salt water filled her mouth as she slipped beneath the waves. Pinwheeling, she burst to the surface and spat.

Cold seeped directly into her skin. Oh, God, I'm going to drown! Please, please, don't let me drown. She heard a meow. "Boots!" She splashed over to the cat. "Hang on to me!" she said.

Boots latched onto her sweater. She sank into the waves and kicked herself back up. "Watch the claws!" she said. "Which way is shore?"

"I don't know! I can't see land!" the cat howled.

Think. Don't panic. Just don't panic. Trying to imagine the sea as Northcourt Pool, she started breaststroking. Waves broke against her. Her side cramped almost instantly. Her arms began to ache. She'd never make it. It was too far. It was endless. It was impossible.

Now she remembered she'd once seen her mom scared. Julie was younger, in elementary school, and she and Gillian were trying to ice-skate on the pond behind Gillian's house. Except the water wasn't fully frozen. Her mom came outside just as the ice first cracked.

A swell shoved into her, and Julie went under. She came up sputtering. "I don't want to drown!" Boots cried. "I'm too young to drown! I've never had kittens! I've never even had a girlfriend!"

Swells crashed into them, dunking them. Boots dug his claws into her back and yowled at the waves.

Chapter Sixteen
Swan Soldiers

She felt a yank on her hair, and her face was jerked above the waves. Julie gasped for air. It burned. Oh, it burned! Something clamped onto her elbows and then onto her legs. Horizontal, she was raised out of the ocean.

Suspended an inch over the water, she started moving forward with a *whoosh* sound. Her stomach skimmed the surface of the sea. Waves slapped her face. She rose higher. *Whoosh, whoosh*, she heard. What was happening?

Out of the corner of her eye, she caught a glimpse of white. Held by the hair, she couldn't move her head. "Boots! Boots, where are you?" she called.

She heard the cat's voice: "Don't eat me! Please, don't eat me! I swear I'll never chase another sparrow. Not even a chickadee!"

She heard a louder *whoosh*. Feathers filled her view—she was in a flock of giant swans. Each bird was at least six feet long from beak to tail feathers. The closest swan turned its boa neck toward her. "Don't worry, miss. Everything's under control. We said we'd look out for you, and here we are," the swan said. "Lieutenant, loosen up on that hair there."

Lieutenant . . . She knew them! She'd seen them turned into swans: they were the National Guardsmen she'd met back on Main Street.

The lieutenant holding her hair loosened his grip, and she turned her head to see a man-sized swan holding her elbow in his beak. "Where are you taking us?" she called.

The lead swan flapped ahead without answering. "Keep up that V formation, boys! Let me see those wings flap! What are you, a bunch of sissies? Up, down. Up, down!"

Ocean passed underneath her as the swans flew on.

*   *   *

"Gently, gently. On three: one, two . . ." The swans lowered her toward a patch of moss. Two inches from the ground, the swans released her and she belly-flopped onto the ground.

She lifted her face. "Ow," she said.

In a flutter of wings, the swans landed around her. She pushed herself to her knees. Beside her, Boots lay shuddering on the ground. She crawled to him. "Are you okay?" she asked.

"Birds," he said. "Giant birds."

"But are you okay?"

He raised his head and looked at her. Fur wet, his face looked like a mop. "I'm wet," he said. "I'm cold. I'm hungry."

She hugged him. "Yeah, me too," she said. He didn't squirm out of her arms. Instead, he curled against her as she looked around them. They were on a shore, a narrow beach of rocks lined by the encroaching forest. The swans were waddling in between the trees toward a picturesque cottage. "Excuse me, uh, sir?" she called. "Where are we?"

"Safe," said the closest swan, the captain. "You'll stay here for the night." On the word *night*, the sky suddenly tinted orange. Julie and Boots looked up. Across the water, the afternoon sun had dipped instantly into sunset.

Okay, that was disturbing. Her urge to leave the Wild suddenly doubled. "Sir? We were heading for an ogre's castle. It's supposed to be on the other side of the ocean."

"Step lively, men," the captain barked. The swans waddled toward the cottage. As they approached it, they seemed to stretch and darken. Their wings shrank and thinned. Their legs extended. One by one, their feathers faded into army green fatigues, and their beaks flattened into human faces.

"They're human only in the evenings until the spell is broken," Boots whispered. Julie nodded, remembering the story: someone had to sew eleven shirts of flowers to turn them human again. She and Boots watched the soldiers march into the cottage. "Hope you like sewing," Boots said.

"You don't think . . ." She couldn't be caught in another story so quickly! She looked at the captain. "Um, sir, I don't have time to break your spell. I have to get to—"

"We already have someone sewing," the captain said.

Wow, that was lucky. "You do?"

"Of course," he said. "Come meet her. She's in the tree." Boots leapt out of her arms as Julie followed the captain around the cottage. In the space of time it took them to walk no more than thirty steps, the sun set and the moon rose. All the trees were dark masses of shadows.

Julie shivered and walked closer to the captain. She'd thought the woods were terrifying in daylight. She hadn't imagined them in the dark. In the dark, the twisted trunks looked even more like faces. Knots stretched into silent screams. Switching on his flashlight, the captain focused the beam on a tree with a shape in it.

Even though she was expecting it, Julie took a step backward: there was a girl in the tree. She was making a strange clicking sound.

The captain strode toward her and Julie followed. Light spilled up the tree, illuminating feet, knees, and then hands moving in concert with the clicking—knitting, Julie guessed. As the light hit the knitter's face, the girl lifted her head and flipped her hair to the side. Mouth open, Julie stared at her. Oh, wow.

The girl in the tree was Kristen March.

Kristen's mouth curled, and Julie's shoulders tensed. Kristen recognized her. Like the soldiers, she was in a tale, but unlike New Little Red, she hadn't reached an ending yet. She still had her memories. Lucky me, Julie thought. Kristen was going to say something awful. She knew it.

But Kristen said nothing. Her hands kept moving, the needles kept clicking, and she didn't speak. Why didn't she say something snide? Julie had never known Kristen to resist an insult. But Kristen just kept pulling in blue and red daisies and knitting them together. Of course, Julie thought, the spell! She couldn't talk or laugh while she knit flower shirts for the swan-men. The Wild was forcing her silent, just like it had forced the griffin to buck Julie and Boots. Julie started to laugh. How perfect! Kristen couldn't talk!

The captain looked at Julie curiously. "Do you know her?"

"Yes, I know her." Smiling, she added, "Unfortunately." Kristen's eyes bulged.

"You should be glad she can't talk," Julie said. The pressure of holding in so many snide comments was probably intense. "There are kids at school who would give anything to see her like this."

Kristen's mouth formed an *o* in an almost-hiccup. Her hands moved faster, needles clacking louder.

"She thinks she's so high and mighty," Julie said. "Not

so clever with the insults now, are you? Not so great stuck in a tree by yourself without all your friends around you. Oh, look, I think you missed a row."

Concerned, the captain leaned in. "She has to knit them perfectly, or we'll be swans forever."

Julie waggled her finger at Kristen. "Not so fun being not quite perfect, is it? Bet it'll take you a long time to knit these."

"Six years," the captain said.

Julie stopped. Six years? She stared at the soldier. Did he mean it? Even Kristen didn't deserve . . . but no, she did deserve it. Julie thought of how many days she had gone home in tears, hating herself because of Kristen. Who knew how many other lives she'd ruined? But six years . . . Julie turned back to Kristen. Kristen knit furiously.

The captain clapped his hand on Julie's shoulder. "Let's go inside."

He led Julie across the clearing. Julie kept glancing back over her shoulder until Kristen was swallowed in darkness.

* * *

Julie tossed on the cot. It wasn't really night; she couldn't sleep. Besides, each time she closed her eyes, she could feel the seawater closing over her. She'd been lucky.

Lucky. Oh, yes, she'd been lucky: she'd met the animal

helpers before she met the witch; Boots had come to guide her to the griffin; the swans had appeared before she drowned . . . Sure, "lucky." She was no different from Kristen, sewing silently in the tree. She was following the Wild's script—just like Kristen and Grandma and New Little Red—and the Wild could twist the plot any way it pleased.

Curling into a ball, she squeezed her pillow. The Wild would never let her succeed. It wouldn't want her to rescue her mother, the one person who knew how to defeat it. It wouldn't want to be put back under Julie's bed.

Except that she wasn't dealing with a malicious mind plotting against her. The Wild had rules, events, conventions. Her eyes flew open, wide awake, as the idea came to her. Instead of trying to escape the stories, she should be trying to live them.

Yes, that was the way to win: follow the tales to the happily ever after of her mother's rescue. Play the role of the hero in a rescue tale—and avoid the role of evil stepsister who spits toads and has her eyes pecked out by talking birds. She might not be able to avoid being in the tales altogether, but she could try to be in the right ones.

Could she do it? She turned the idea over in her head. From what she'd seen and learned, she didn't think that the Wild could control her *between* story bits, just during them. Between events, she had freedom. She could use those moments to find the tales that would lead her to the ending she wanted: her mother's rescue. It could work. Boots had talked once about all the story bits being jumbled because the Wild was growing. He'd used that to avoid his story. Couldn't she use that to *choose* her story?

Julie tossed off the thin blanket. At the foot of the bed, Boots burrowed into her discarded blanket with a contented purr. She took a flashlight and went outside.

Outside, the darkness seemed to close in on her. Nervously, she peered at the shadows. Now that she was out here, she wasn't sure what had prompted her to come outside. What was she trying to prove? Was she trying to prove something?

The darkness retreated to nibble at the edges of her light. Cautiously, she walked across the clearing. Halfway, she heard the clacking sound. She followed it. She raised the flashlight and the light fell on Kristen, knitting in the tree.

Kristen lifted her head and looked at her, and then Julie understood what had made her come outside. "I'm going to end this," Julie said. "You won't have to do this for six years."

Kristen raised her eyebrows. Julie recognized that expression: disbelief. "Look, I know more about this than you do. You're just going to have to trust me."

Kristen's nostrils flared: disgust.

"You might know how to deal with the school world better than I do. But all your perfection out there doesn't help you in here. You know what's going to happen to you next if you continue with this set of events? You'll knit in silence for five and a half years, and then some king will come along and marry you. You'll have kids. Your mother-in-law will kill them and tell the king you ate them. And then you'll be tied to a stake to burn. Bet you didn't know that."

Julie warmed to her subject: "You don't know enough to avoid the wrong roles. And Grandma and the others know too much." It was beginning to make sense. Gothel and "our kind" had roles here, so they were trapped quickly. Kristen and the others didn't know enough to avoid the roles, so they were also trapped quickly. Julie was the only one who could recognize the story bits *and* who didn't already belong to a specific story. "I'm the only one who straddles both worlds," Julie said.

Kristen tossed her hair, and Julie suddenly remembered who she was talking to. She scowled at Kristen. "Well, it doesn't matter if you appreciate it or not. I'm not doing it for you." Julie stomped away. She went back inside and woke the soldiers. "My brother and I need to get to the ogre's castle."

Chapter Seventeen
Cat-and-Mouse Games

Julie knelt on the swan's back and held on to his neck. Powerful wings pumped beneath her. She glanced back at Boots. He was huddled between the wings of the swan lieutenant. She waved back at him, and he bared his teeth. "Unnatural!" he shouted. "A cat riding a bird!"

Grinning, she turned forward. On the horizon, the sun was rising, sparkling and dancing on the water. It was a beautiful morning in every way. She was going to Mom! She was going home!

The swans skimmed low over the surface of the sea. Spray spattered in Julie's face. She laughed out loud as the swan burst through a puff of sea mist. She saw Worcester's Higgins Armory Museum in the distance.

Its steel windows stretched like taffy into thin, delicate silver walls. It towered fifty stories in the air with turrets that reached into the clouds. Its sparkle filled Julie's eyes. Silver reflected on the blue sea.

The swans glided onto the parking-lot-turned-shore. One of the swans gestured grandly with his wing and said, "Here is the Castle of the Silver Towers."

Yes, that seemed a better name for it now. Awed, she stared up at the shining turrets. "We used to come here for field trips," she said. "It didn't look like this." It used to be shorter, for one thing, and she was sure it hadn't had a moat or a drawbridge. Or an ogre.

Suddenly, the castle didn't seem so wonderful. She remembered her mom once casually mentioning how different the Giant-Ogre family was outside the Wild. Gothel had used her magic to shrink them. Outside the Wild, one of them could eat six steaks for dinner. Inside the Wild, that same ogre could eat a whole herd of cattle.

Boots leapt down from the swan lieutenant's back.

The swan screeched. "My feathers!"

"Sorry," Boots said. Not looking the least bit sorry, he smiled with a feather in between his fangs.

"Boots!" What was he thinking? They were their ride! She dismounted and then turned to apologize, but the swans were already back in V formation. "Hey, where are you going?"

The swans didn't answer. Instead, she heard the captain's voice across the water, drilling them to fly faster. Soon, they were specks in the distance; then they were gone. So much for their escape route. "Good job, Boots," she said. Swallowing hard, she turned back to the castle.

"I don't suppose it's a friendly ogre?"

"You go ahead," he said, lifting his leg to lick his boot. "I'll guard the entrance."

"Nice try," she said. She picked him up. She was *not* doing this alone.

Squirming out of her arms, he climbed onto her shoulder. "I want an extra can of Fancy Feast for this."

Julie crossed the drawbridge to the door. Ornate gold, the door sparkled like sequins. It was ten times as tall as Julie. She squinted up at the door handle, which was the equivalent of three stories above her. "Do you think I should knock?" she asked.

"I wouldn't," Boots said, leaping off her shoulder.

Julie pushed on the door. It didn't budge. "Why not?" she asked.

"An ogre might answer," he said.

Cute. She rolled her eyes at him. "What would Mom do?" Two days ago, she would have thought she knew the answer: her mother wouldn't be on a quest. But today . . . who knew? Maybe Mom would lay siege to the castle and take the ogre single-handed. Yeah, right.

Gathering her courage, Julie knocked on the door. She thought her knock sounded like the tap of a small wood-pecker. She knocked harder. "Ow." She winced and shook her hand, knuckles stinging. She rubbed her fingers and then knocked again.

Thud.

Julie took a step backward. *Thud, thud, thud.* Door hinges shivered. Gold bits broke from the facade and rained down on them. Julie retreated down the draw-bridge and wished she hadn't knocked. She should have found her own way to Mom instead of following this stu-pid story. She heard a clank, and the massive door swung open. A Volkswagen-sized boot slammed down in the doorway, followed by a second boot. Julie tilted her head back: ankle, calf, knee, up and up until she finally saw the ogre's face, five stories above her. He scowled down at her. "Fee, fie, foe, fum! I smell the blood of an Englishmun!"

Julie swallowed hard. Coming here, she thought, was a stupid, stupid idea. "Actually, I'm American. And a girl."

"Eh?" The ogre peered down at her, and then he squat-ted, enormous knees jutting forward, for a better look. "Ooh, so you are! Like a tiny doll."

Look at the size of his hands. He could crush her like an ant. "Yep, that's me. A doll, not an Englishmun. I mean, Englishman. And this is my brother, Puss-in-Boots."

"Leave me out of this," Boots said out of the corner of his mouth.

The ogre spread his hands apologetically. "Unfor-tunately, this changes nothing. You are still human." He straightened to his full height and thundered: "Be he alive or be he dead, I'll grind his bones to make my bread!" The drawbridge throbbed with the volume of his voice. Julie clapped her hands to her ears. "Why have you entered my domain?"

Good question—what had she been thinking? How did storybook heroes ever escape him? A memory of a story tickled her mind: something about a cat and a carnivorous ogre. Try it, her mind whispered. It couldn't possibly make things worse. "Because I heard of your awesome powers," she squeaked.

He smiled, exposing hubcap-sized yellow teeth. "You've heard of me?"

"Oh, yes." Please, let this be the right story. She didn't want to be crushed. She didn't want to be eaten. "I heard that you could change shapes."

"Yes, I am all-powerful!" roared the ogre.

Leaning close to her ankle, Boots said, "Julie, what are you doing?"

Julie shook the cat off her foot. "Play along," she whispered to him. "I heard that you can turn into a dragon," she said to the ogre, "but I didn't believe it. Who could turn into something as great as a dragon?"

Boots covered his head with his paws. "Oh, no. Don't bait him."

"You doubt my power? I will prove it to you!" With his thumb and forefinger, he drew a tiny stick from his pocket.

He tapped himself with it. "From an ogre to a dragon!"

Suddenly, he bulged. His stomach distended and his arms flattened. His torso elongated and turned green. Scales burst out over his skin. His face lengthened into jaws, and his eyes narrowed into yellow slits. His hands curled into claws.

Julie swallowed twice. She felt like Jell-O. How had she thought it couldn't get worse? This was obviously worse. If Mom was such a great hero, why couldn't she save herself this time too? Why was it up to Julie? She didn't belong here. She just wanted to go home. Boots quivered behind her.

Spitting tendrils of fire, the dragon pranced around the castle foyer. His claws echoed on the tile. "Can you deny I am the most powerful creature you've ever seen?" he said. Sword-sharp teeth flashed.

Staring at his jaws, she couldn't find her voice. She wet her lips. "I'm . . . impressed." Her knees shook. She closed her eyes and said in a rush, "But it's not so hard to make yourself bigger. What would be really impressive is if you could make yourself smaller, like a dog or a cat or even a mouse."

"I can do that!" With the wand in his claw, he tapped himself again. "From a dragon to a mouse!" His green skin grayed, and his bones shrank. His body collapsed inward. In seconds, a mouse sat on top of the wand.

"Aha!" Puss-in-Boots pounced on the mouse, knocking the wand out of his claws. Julie pounced on the wand. The mouse-ogre squealed.

Yes! Julie clutched the wand to her chest. Her hands shook. Before she lost her nerve, she said, "Now, Mr. Ogre, if I turn you back, will you promise to behave and take us to the magician?"

Boots licked his muzzle. "Don't promise. I'm hungry."

The mouse shivered and squeaked, "I promise! Promise!"

He had to keep his promise, right? The Wild wouldn't let him lie. "Stand back," she told the cat. Boots backed away from the mouse, and Julie touched the mouse's nose with the wand. "From a mouse to an ogre."

The mouse grew into the ogre. "Good show," the ogre said. "Nicely done."

Not trusting her voice, she nodded thanks. Her heart rate slowly returned to normal. She tucked the wand in her back pocket.

"Would you like that ride now?" the ogre asked. He held down his hand.

Julie hesitated for a second. What if he closed his hand on her? Stay brave, she told herself. You're almost to Mom. It's almost over. Picking up the cat, Julie climbed onto his palm. The ogre lifted them to face level. "Um, sorry about earlier," he said. "Part of the rules, you know."

"I know. You wouldn't really have eaten me."

The ogre looked embarrassed. "Actually, I would have. But don't worry, I'd have cooked you first."

* * *

Julie and Boots rode on the rim of the ogre's hat as he trampled the trees beyond the castle. "You know, I fought by your mother's side in the Great Battle," the ogre said, after introductions had been made.

Surprised, Julie almost lost her grip on the hat. "It's true? She was in a battle?" she asked eagerly.

"She led the battle," the ogre corrected. "And she organized all the attempts before that. She was the leader of the rebellion since its inception. Your mother was a great swordswoman."

"Swords? Mom?" Mom, who always yelled at her to be careful with scissors and knives—Mom was a swordswoman? Wow. What else? She had to know it all.

"She learned in her tower," the ogre said, "trained visit by visit by her prince—or so the story goes. She was the inspiration of many a knight in shining armor."

"Why didn't you tell me any of this?" Julie asked Boots. When he opened his mouth, she added, "*Before* yesterday." She had lived with Boots all her life, and he had never said a word. He'd kept this all a mystery.

"Do *you* like to dredge up all of your least favorite

memories?" he asked. "Besides, she wanted to leave this behind, and it wasn't my story to tell."

No, it was Mom's story.

Mom should have been the one to tell her. Julie felt . . . She didn't know how she felt. Mom had kept secrets from her. She'd kept secrets from her own daughter.

Five centuries ago, Mom had written in her own blood, ridden a griffin into battle, and led a rebellion. And Julie never knew.

It hurt.

Julie wasn't even sure she knew the woman who had been described to her. She thought of her mom in the kitchen the other morning, laughing, applying makeup, baby-talking with her ridiculous "oobe snooby uppy wuppy." How did this mom mesh with the warrior?

Julie looked out across the landscape—hints of highways and houses buried under green—and tried to imagine how the Wild Wood had looked to Mom five hundred years ago. Mom had led a rebellion in order to leave her past behind. Julie tried to wrap her mind around this new image of her mother. Mom had masterminded the escape from the Wild.

And now she was back in it, and it was growing. Had it taken over all of Massachusetts? Did it control all of New England? How fast was it growing, and how much of its speed was due to Julie feeding it with her rescue stories? I'll find you, Mom, she promised herself. I'll set it right. "I think that's Route 9," Julie called to Boots. White City Cinemas had transformed into an ivory castle, and Stop 'n' Shop was a peasant town. McDonald's now had a thatched roof.

The ogre laid his hat on the ground. Julie and Boots lowered themselves over the lip of the felt. "He'll be asleep now," the ogre said. "You'd better hurry."

"Can't you help us get it?" Julie asked.

"Oh, no, you already have a companion," he said. "Besides, I have to be going. Villages to terrorize. Peasants to eat. Ahh, I've missed this—at least the parts until I'm murdered." Waving, the ogre stomped off, squashing a Hallmark hut and Ye Olde Blockbuster Shoppe.

Julie faced Spag's warehouse store. Through the cobweb-coated, bat-lined door, all she saw was a whole lot of darkness. "You first," she said to Boots.

"No, no, please, be my guest," Boots said.

Julie poked a finger at a cobweb. It broke and clung to her finger. Ew.

You can do it, Julie, she told herself. She was so close now. One more of the Wild's stupid games and she would be with Mom. If Mom could wield a sword in battle, Julie could get one measly ring from a magician. After all, it wasn't as if she'd be the one facing down the Wild. Covering her face with her hands, she walked quickly into the cobwebs and through the revolving door. Cobwebs stuck to her hands, her arms, her legs, her hair. On the other side, she wiped them off as quickly as she could. Yuck, yuck, and very yuck.

Rubbing her arms, she looked around her. It wasn't completely black inside the store-cave. Sconces with torches lit the walls instead of the normal fluorescent bulbs. Flickering shadows stretched across the hardware section. Under a layer of moss and lichen, paint cans still sat on shelves and drill bits in open drawers.

"Spooky," Boots commented.

Julie agreed. The shadows looked like they could hold dozens of monsters. "Let's go," she whispered to Boots. She crept forward into the aisles.

Silently, they passed the jewelry cases. Her image flickered in dusty mirrors. She watched out of the corner of her eye as her image followed them into the cookware aisle.

Boots sniffed the air. "Up ahead," he whispered.

She crept as quietly as she could, following the cat through electronics. The VCRs looked like black blotches. Anything could be hiding behind the TVs. Coming out of electronics, she heard a soft rumble.

She imagined monsters: drooling, bloodthirsty monsters.

Julie and Boots crept through patio furniture. Fast asleep, the magician was facedown on a patio table. His cheek was smushed against the glass next to the umbrella hole and his half-eaten lunch, and he was snoring—the soft rumble she'd heard was his snoring.

"That's him?" Julie said. *That* was the magician? He was a kid. He looked high school age. Pimples and everything. He wore a Harry Potter wizard hat and a blue bathrobe with stars and moons on it. The hat still had a price tag.

"Shhh!" Boots said, but the magician didn't wake.

"Come on," she whispered. Dropping to hands and knees, she crawled closer. She hid behind a barbecue grill. Boots joined her. "Grandma said he keeps it in his mouth," Julie whispered. Leaning around the grill, she peeked out at the kid. His mouth was shut. His nostrils flared with each snore.

How could she make him spit out the ring in his sleep? What would make someone spit in his sleep? Or how about sneeze? What would make him sneeze?

"Cat hair," she said.

"Excuse me?" Boots said.

She grinned at Boots. "You can make him sneeze."

"Um, let me think about that: magician, me. Uh, no. Absolutely not."

"Come on," she whispered. "You said you wanted to go home."

He backed away. "It's not *that* bad here. You heard the ogre—he missed parts of this place. Who knows? Maybe I gave up too early before. Maybe if I stick around, I will meet the love of my life. If I'm magician lunch meat, I'll never know."

She couldn't believe he was talking like this. "What about Mom?"

"She's a hero," Boots said. "I'm just the hero's companion."

Julie shook her head. "You almost drowned, you flew on swans, you faced an ogre, you followed me in here, and *now* you want to back out?"

"This is where I draw the line," he said. "Besides, maybe he's not allergic to cat hair."

"Okay, fine," she said. She wasn't going to waste time arguing with him. "What else makes people sneeze?"

"Dust," he suggested. "Pepper?"

The magician had been eating a submarine sandwich from the food aisle. His hand rested in a soggy mass of shredded lettuce and ham remnants. She bet it had pepper.

She couldn't waltz over to him and stick pepper in his nose without his noticing. He'd hear her. If Boots would do it . . . or an even smaller creature . . . Yes! "Wait here," Julie whispered. "I have an idea."

She pulled the ogre's wand out of her back pocket. Taking a deep breath, she tapped her head with its tip. "From a girl to a mouse."

Whoosh. She shot toward the floor, and the barbecue grill ballooned in front of her. Heavy and awkward, the wand fell out of her hands as her fingers curled into paws. Her back slouched as her bones shifted. Her skin itched as she sprouted fur. Her nose twitched, her whiskers moved, and she was suddenly assailed by more smells than she'd ever imagined existed. She swallowed back a cough, tried to cover her mouth with her front paws, and fell flat on her chin.

Paws scrabbling, she righted herself. Gingerly, she laid her tail straight out behind her. She looked down at herself. Wow, wait until she told Gillian about this. Gillian would love it. She'd say it was super-cool—and she'd be right, Julie thought. "Boots, look at me!" She lifted her head and twitched her whiskers.

Oh, my, he was huge. And feline.

Boots towered over her, lashing his tail. "I want Beef Feast for the self-restraint I am showing here." His teeth glittered.

Julie bolted for the patio furniture. Her hind haunches waddled faster than her front, and she somersaulted over the linoleum. Adjusting herself, she zigzagged toward the magician's table. Okay, here's the plan, she thought as she ran: I climb up the table leg . . .

At the foot of the table leg, she looked up—and up and up. Okay, here's the plan: I *don't* climb up the table leg . . . She waddled to the magician's robe. Oversized, it draped onto the floor in a puddle of terry cloth.

A mouse could climb this, she thought.

Before she lost her nerve, Julie dug her front paws into the cloth and scrabbled behind her with her hind claws. She started to climb. Memories flashed back at her: how she hated gym class, how she hated jungle gyms.

Suddenly, the mountain leveled off. She had reached the magician's thigh. She looked down—a long, long way down—and bit back a squeak. Paws clenched on the robe, her legs shook. The linoleum swam beneath her. She clung to the terry cloth. Her mouse heart pattered like a snare drum. What a terrible idea this was. She couldn't do it. She wasn't a mouse acrobat.

She had been much higher in the ogre's hat and on the griffin's back, she told herself. After a long minute, she was able to move again. She gritted her mouse teeth and continued her climb: up the front lapel of the bathrobe and along the sleeve. She focused on one inch at a time. Concentrating, she forgot to be afraid.

Before she knew it, she was at the table. She scurried across the magician's arm and onto the table, landing with a sharp click of claws on glass.

Oh, wow, she did it. She couldn't believe she did it. She looked down. The frosted glass table warped her view of the floor below. She saw Boots watching her, and she waved with her tail. He flicked his tail in the air as if snapping a whip.

She hurried around the magician's head. His pimples were the size of anthills. His nostrils widened like sails as he breathed. The wind of his breath ruffled her fur. She sniffed at his sandwich.

Yes! He'd used pepper. She dipped her tail into the olive oil smeared on the bread and then rolled her tail in pepper; then she scurried over to the magician. Leaning onto her front paws, she stuck her peppery tail up his nostril. She wiggled it.

The magician sneezed, and the hurricane blew her across the table. She tumbled, paws over tail. The ring clanged as it hit the table and rolled. He snorted. Scrambling her paws under her, Julie ran for the ring. As it tipped toward the edge, she caught it.

The magician rubbed his nose, and his eyelashes fluttered.

Ring in her mouth, Julie ran for the umbrella hole in the patio table. She dove through and slid on her stomach down the table leg. Crashing onto the ground, she oomphed, and the ring fell out of her mouth and clattered on the tile. The magician shifted above her. "Wha . . . wha . . ." he said. She bit the ring and ran across the floor toward the barbecue grill. Butting her head against the wand, she squeaked, "From a mouse to a girl!"

She popped back into her original size.

The magician lifted his head. "Hey, who . . ." Spitting

out the ring, she shoved it on her finger. Boots tucked the ogre's wand into his boot and leapt into Julie's arms.

"Take me to my mother," she shouted at the ring. "Take me to Rapunzel!" The magician charged up the aisle—and the store vanished.

Part Three

The Well

Chapter Eighteen
The Problem with Short Hair

For the thousandth time, Zel peered out the window. The view hadn't changed much since she'd been imprisoned here. Occasionally, a beanstalk rose and fell. Once in a while, a glass hill appeared. Earlier, she had seen a giant-ogre stride across the landscape. Leaning out over the sill, she scanned the horizon for any hint of the one thing she wanted to see: if the Wild had trapped Julie.

Julie wasn't the third son or the youngest of seven daughters. She didn't have butter-yellow hair or skin as plastic smooth as Barbie's. What would the Wild make her be? What if she was forced to play a stepsister? Or a stepmother? Or a serving maid who displaced a princess?

Breathe, Zel told herself. Most likely, one of the others had saved her. Julie could be in Florida with the fairy godmother right now. Or she could be in Cindy's car, fleeing across the Midwest. She could be at a McDonald's in Indiana.

Or she could be trapped in a gingerbread house.

Or inside a wolf's stomach.

Or at the bottom of a well.

Zel resumed her pacing. She hated this. She had hated it centuries ago, and she hated it now. All she could do in this idiotic tower was think and worry. She wanted to scream. She wanted to hurl herself at the Wild and tear it apart branch by branch.

Been there; tried that. Was she doomed to repeat it all? Would she ever see her daughter again? She thought of her husband, and suddenly it hurt to swallow. It could happen, she realized. She could lose them both. She wouldn't get to see Julie grow up. She'd never see her graduate. She'd never attend her daughter's wedding. She would never see the time come when Julie was ready to be friends, not just mother and daughter. Some idiot had made a wish and, in seconds, taken it all away from her.

No, not an idiot: someone who knew exactly when Gothel would be away from the well, someone who knew the three bears would be guarding it, someone who knew their habits and weaknesses. All the evidence pointed to one of their own kind. But how could anyone who knew this world as it truly was want to return to it? No matter how many years passed, no matter how bad their lives were outside the Wild, how could anyone forget that "fairy-tale perfect" was a lie? Maybe an ordinary person, someone who didn't know firsthand, could glorify the Wild Wood, but Zel could not imagine how bad life would have to be to knowingly choose this endless oblivion—and to knowingly condemn everyone to this hell. Yes, hell. Zel closed her eyes and took a deep, ragged breath, trying to stay calm. It couldn't be one of their own who did this. She knew that much.

Beyond that, she knew little else. After she'd tried and failed to call Ursa, Gothel had left for the motel. She had told Zel to stay home with Julie. Most likely, there wasn't a problem, she'd said. But when she didn't report back, Zel followed her—and arrived too late. The Wild had already begun to grow. Zel knocked on every door and evacuated all the guests she could find; then she went into the motel office, where she found the three bears asleep over the drugged porridge. Gothel was nowhere to be seen. Zel went out the back door into the overnight-ancient forest, intending to go straight to the well and undo the damage. But the Wild, of course, had other plans, and Gothel dragged her off to a tower. Just like old times.

At first, the "tower" was nothing more than the motel office, its doors and windows sealed with vines. But the Wild grew fast, and soon she was taken to the top floor of the old town hall, then to the steeple of the Unitarian Church, then to the clock tower of the Worcester courthouse. Finally, the Wild moved her here, to a place that seemed custom-made for her, the Shakespeare in the Park tower. Built to resemble a miniature feudal castle, it already had a turret, arrow slots, and a portcullis when the Wild came. All the Wild had to do was add another three levels and seal the doors into solid stone, and the park monument made a perfect Rapunzel's tower. It would remain usable for centuries with minimal additional effort from the Wild. The Wild would barely have to change anything for Zel to reenact her story. How convenient. How expedient. How lucky.

Zel heard a pop from outside. What was that? Was it the witch already? Please, not yet. She wasn't ready yet. She crossed the room in three steps. "Is anyone there?" She looked out the window.

"Mom?" she heard.

No, it couldn't be. Zel leaned out the window so far that her feet lifted off the floor. "Julie?"

Julie came running around the corner of the tower with Boots behind her. He was in full Puss-in-Boots regalia, and he had a wand poking out of one boot. She was in ordinary jeans and a sweater, plus those ridiculous sandals. "Mom!" she shouted.

"Julie!" She could have wept. Her daughter, here, in the flesh . . . in the Wild. "What are you doing here? You should be miles and miles from the woods! Why didn't you run?"

"I came to rescue you!" Julie said.

Oh, no.

On his hind legs, Boots waved up at her. "Hello, Rapunzel!"

Julie called, "Let down your hair, Mom!"

"Oh, Julie," Zel said. "I cut my hair five centuries ago."

She watched her daughter's smile fall. It felt like a fist in her heart. "But the witch said the ogre . . . and then the magician . . . I crossed the endless ocean! I did the impossible tasks! I won the ring!" Julie held up her hand, but her finger was bare. With its use, the ring had disintegrated. "It's gone!"

Zel closed her eyes. "Oh, pumpkin, you've been tricked. You've been used. The Wild used you for its stories." Just like old times. Only in the old days, it hadn't been her daughter that it had in its grip.

All the pain, all the loss—the whole escape had been to save Julie. Zel had done it all so her child wouldn't grow up a slave to the stories, so she could be her own person. She had even asked Gothel to use her magic to delay Julie's birth until she was sure they were free. We *were* free, she thought. It wasn't fair.

Julie should have run. What had she been thinking, playing hero? She was just a little girl. Zel's little girl.

Zel opened her eyes and looked out again, afraid she was gone. Hands clenched, Julie was staring at the forest. Zel felt déjà vu as she watched the transformation come over her daughter. Julie's back straightened and her chin lifted. She looked up at her mother with a fierce expression on her face, an expression that Zel had never seen her wear. For an instant, Julie reminded her of herself. Was that how she'd looked when she'd fought against the Wild? "How do I stop it?" Julie said.

"You don't," Zel said firmly. "You get out of here. Run as far away as you can."

Just as firmly, Julie said, "I'm not leaving you."

"It's too dangerous." Believe me, she thought. I know what I'm talking about. She'd seen the horrors: red-hot iron shoes, barrels full of nails. Once, she'd seen a woman thrown into a cauldron of vipers. "I want you to leave these woods."

"How? It's not going to let me waltz out."

Julie was right. For a long moment, Zel stared out of the tower at the vast expanse of the Wild Wood. She'd been in the woods for hundreds of years before she was able to face the Wild. Julie was only twelve. But twelve or not, the Wild would make her a character, and there was only one character she could be if she wanted to escape. "You'll have to hurry," Zel said. "The Wild is in chaos now because it's growing. But the same chaos that makes it possible to switch from story to story also makes it possible for the Wild to present you with trap after trap. The longer you take, the more chances the Wild will have to surround you with stories—eventually, it will trick you into a story ending, and you'll forget who you are. That's how we lost the Great Battle. You will have to move quickly, and you can't stop. And above all else, *you must avoid story endings.*"

"Where do I go?" Julie asked.

"You need to make a wish," Zel said. "You need to go to the Wishing Well Motel and make a wish. But it has to be the wish that's dearest to your heart or the Wild will find a way to make it come out wrong."

"I'll do it, Mom," Julie promised.

"You have to beat the Wild at its own game. It's the only way to defeat it," Zel said. Battles, tricks, persuasion, none of it had worked. "The Wild has to play by its own rules. Remember that."

"I will," Julie said. "I love you, Mom!"

Zel's throat clogged. There were a thousand things she wanted to say . . . First was: Don't go. Sending her daughter off . . . She'd already lost her husband; she couldn't lose Julie too. "Julie . . ."

"Yeah, yeah, I'll be careful."

"Have an uneventful day," her mother said.

Julie waved and plunged back into the forest.

"I love you!" Rapunzel called after her.

The forest swallowed Julie and the cat without a sound.

Chapter Nineteen
Goldilocks and the Beanstalk

Out of the sun and away from her mother, Julie didn't feel so brave. She was in Worcester now—a solid fifteen-minute drive from the Wishing Well Motel, when the highways weren't covered in moss and griffins. At a walk, it would take hours. Lots of opportunities for ogres and witches and wolves to make life difficult. For the first time ever, Julie found herself wishing for Cindy and her Subaru.

"You cannot do this," Boots said flatly.

"Hey, how about a little optimism here?" Reaching down, she scratched under his chin. He didn't purr or tilt his head into her hand. "Boots, what's wrong?"

"You cannot rescue her," he said. "You cannot make this wish."

Jeez, with friends like these . . . "You're on my side, remember? Boots?" He didn't respond. Staring straight ahead, he sat stiff like a stuffed doll. "Boots? You okay?"

Mechanically he raised his head to look at her like he was a puppet controlled by strings. She shivered. Something wasn't right. "Boots?" She had the sudden irrational thought that this wasn't Boots. "Are you . . . Who are you?" she asked.

"I am the heart of the fairy tale," the Wild said, through the mouth of her brother.

Oh, no. No, it couldn't be. Julie rocked backward. The Wild wasn't alive. It didn't have a mind. Grandma, Goldie . . . everyone had said it was a force. Like gravity. Mom had never said it was alive. She'd never said it could do this.

"This story must not be. You must find another," the Wild said. "You will ruin everything."

The Wild was alive. It was alive, and it was speaking through Boots. She turned and ran. "Mom, Mom!" She wove between trunks. Behind each tree was another and another and another . . . Panting, she slowed. The tower was gone. She turned in a circle—thick trees in all directions . . .

The cat sat on the path.

Julie yelped. "Go away. Leave me alone."

"I am offering a gift: the world as it should be."

She shook her head. That made no sense. *None* of this made sense. She was talking to the forest? She was talking to the fairy tale? "This is crazy," she said. "You're destroying people."

"On the contrary," it said. "I am giving them meaning."

She didn't understand.

"I give them a beginning, a middle, and an end; a once upon a time and a happily ever after. I give rewards to the good and punishment to the bad. I give order and sense to an otherwise arbitrary existence."

Oh, God, she thought, it's crazy. The forest was insane.

With her brother's paw, the Wild gestured at the shadowy trees. "In here, life is fair. Everyone has a place. Everyone belongs." With her brother's eyes, it looked at Julie. Its eyes were matte black. "I am offering you what you've always wanted, Julie Marchen. You can belong here."

Anger flashed through Julie so fast that it made her shake. "You don't know anything about me or what I want. You put my mom in a tower. You made me grow up without a dad . . ." She swallowed hard as her voice cracked.

"This is how it must be," it said. "This is how it is."

"Yeah, well, not anymore," she said. "Count me out. Not playing. Game over." She marched past the cat and down the path. She knew it was bravado. How was she going to cross fifteen miles with the Wild actively against her? How was she going to defeat something that wasn't just powerful but was also intelligent? How had Mom done it? What had happened *after* the Great Battle? Julie wished she had asked. Yes, Mom had said to hurry, but Julie should have asked. She'd been stupid.

Maybe all along, she'd been stupid. Had the Wild been watching her the whole time, sabotaging her? Had the Wild made Boots take her to the griffin, knowing the griffin would dump her into the water? Had it made Boots pick up the ogre's wand after she won the ring so that she couldn't use it now? Or was its interference even further back? Was everything a setup? Was this why she had found Boots with the bikes—so the Wild could possess him? Was this why Boots had been able to avoid his story ending? Had the Wild preserved him to be a pawn? She kept walking.

"You can't escape," it said. "Inside me, you play by my rules."

Over her shoulder, she said, "Yeah? Well, so do you." Suddenly, Julie had the answer. She almost laughed out loud. It was absurd, but it just might work. After all, the Wild had to play by its own rules! As far as she knew, its rules did not include fairy-tale princesses breaking their royal promises. "Cindy, I'm calling in your promise! I could use that ride now!"

She only half expected it to work, but pine needles crackled as Cinderella's carriage rolled through the forest and broke out of the bushes onto the path in front of her. The frog-faced coachman reined in the mouse-horses.

Cindy opened the door to the pumpkin and waved. "Joo-lie! Quick, hop in!"

* * *

Inside the carriage, orange goop dripped from the ceiling. Julie sat, and pumpkin slop spurted out from underneath her with a farting sound. Opposite her, Cindy settled her dress in the mush. In place of her normal glitter, she wore a ball gown covered in diamond drops and pearls. The coachman cracked his whip. Neighing, the horses increased speed, and the pumpkin coach bounced through the forest. Julie saw trees whip past them like highway guardrails. He drives like Cindy, Julie thought. Good. She'd get there faster.

Face pinched and worried, Cindy twisted her gloved hands in her lap as if strangling her knuckles. Julie had never seen her look so unhappy. "I can take you most of the way—at least to the center of Northboro," Cindy said. "Beyond that, the Wild will force this carriage to the ball."

Alarm bells rang in Julie's head. "It won't force me, will it?" Could she have walked into a trap?

"*I* won't," Cindy said. "I'm Cinderella. I don't do that sort of thing." Her voice sounded bitter. Julie didn't think she'd ever heard Cindy sound bitter. The coach bounced, and Julie knocked into a wall. Cindy caught herself on the window. "You'd best steer clear of fairies, though. Especially godmothers."

There was a lot she needed to steer clear of. How on

earth was she going to make it to the motel on her own? She swallowed the lump in her throat. She shouldn't have left Boots behind. No matter how the Wild used him, he was still her brother. "You're sure you can't go farther?"

"You were lucky you called me when you did. In a few hours, I'll finish my story and won't remember you. I'll simply be Cinderella again and again and again," Cindy said. She stared out the window at the blur of green. "It's worse this time, being back here. Before, we didn't know for sure there even was a world beyond the Wild. We guessed there was, when the Wild grew and we saw new faces, but we didn't *know*." Her hands were a tight knot on her lap. "It will make them more cruel if they remember what they've lost."

"Who?" Julie asked.

Cindy gave her a sad smile. "Not many people know this, but my stepsisters didn't need the Wild to force them to be cruel. Every time they regained their memories, they hated me anew for their blinding. And I took it, all the work and all the hatred, because how could I blame them? After hundreds and thousands of cycles, there's no way to know what came first: how they treated me or how my birds pecked out their eyes. Now, this time, my new step-sisters will have lost even more than their eyes. Do you know how awful it is to realize that the best-case scenario is that we all forget?"

Julie didn't know how to answer that. What could she

say? Flighty, perky Cindy. Julie had never seen her so . . . so defeated.

"The birds tell me that most of us have already forgotten. Mary. Harp. Gretel." Cindy wilted with each name. At what point would her mother's name join that list? Julie wondered. Sometime soon, a witch would visit Mom in the tower and then a prince . . . Julie had a horrible thought: was another prince going to displace her father?

"Goldie!" Cindy said. Her eyes brightened as if she had a cartoon lightbulb over her head. "Goldie hasn't lost herself yet," Cindy said, excitement in her voice. "She hasn't found three bears to finish her story. Some Pied Piper trumpeter has all the bears dancing. Goldie can help you!" Leaning on the carriage window, Cindy whistled.

Goldie was all that was left? Julie couldn't imagine Goldie helping anyone, except herself, of course. And anyway, what was Goldilocks going to do against the essence of fairy tales?

Julie heard twittering. Sparrows ducked into the carriage. Cindy whistled at them. They sang back. "The birds will find Goldie," Cindy said to Julie. "She can take you the last three miles." Cindy seemed so pleased with herself that Julie could say nothing but "Thanks."

Cindy beamed. "You know, I gave your father a ride like this once upon a time."

Dad? Her heart lurched—the word *father* had caught

her off guard. "You did?" Rapunzel's prince was in a pumpkin carriage?

"He never said why." With a faint frown, Cindy added, "You know, I think that was the last time I saw him."

The last time . . . ? Could Cindy have seen him right before he and Mom stopped the Wild? Julie opened her mouth to ask more, but the carriage ground to a stop. The coachman opened the door and held out a gloved hand to Julie. "I'm sorry I can't take you farther," Cindy said. "Watch out for the seed," she added as Julie stood. "It's a little loose."

Julie looked up. Above her, a three-foot pod hung from an orange thread. "That's a seed?" Ducking under it, Julie climbed out of the carriage.

Cindy leaned on the window. "Joo-lie?" she called.

Julie looked back. "Yes?"

"Hurry," Cinderella said. "Please, hurry."

With a snap of the coachman's whip, the carriage was off, bouncing over roots and moss to disappear between the trees.

* * *

Cindy had let her off in the center of Northboro. Walking quickly, Julie passed the CVS Apothecary, Bank of America Moneylenders, and Dunkin' Donuts (unchanged except for the addition of horse troughs). Rapunzel's Hair Salon had become an old-fashioned barbershop. Refusing to look at it, she walked faster. Where was Goldie?

Hurrying now, she continued down the road, past Shattuck's Pharmacy, which advertised leeches and boil lancers, and past a flower shop that had transformed into a garden with rows of rapunzel greens. Only a few more blocks and she'd be out of the downtown. She passed Northboro House of Pizza, now a medieval bakery.

The street erupted in front of her, and a green sprout burst out of the ground. Leaves peeled off it as the beanstalk thickened. It soared into the clouds. Its top disappeared into white fluff. Julie stumbled backward. When she caught her balance, she moved to go around it. Instead, she found her hand on a leaf.

"Don't climb it!" a voice shouted.

Climb it? She didn't want to climb it. But she lifted her foot onto the base. Someone pulled her by the waist of her jeans, and she lost her grip.

"Ooh, now you've done it." Hands on her hips, Goldie was scowling fiercely—an expression at odds with her curly pigtails and checkerboard frock. Julie shrank back from her scowl. "I bother to come all the way over here on the say-so of Cindy's ridiculous birds, and you're already in trouble," Goldie said.

Crushed, Julie didn't know what to say. It wasn't her fault that the stalk had burst through the sidewalk. "I'm sorry."

Tossing her ringlets, Goldie humphed and turned her glare on the beanstalk. "It's a waste of my time. You'll never make it. You'll never be able to get me out of the Wild," she said. "I'll probably break a nail, and the whole town will see up my skirt. Do you at least know how to stop it?"

It had just sprouted. Julie didn't know where it came from or how to stop it. She looked miserably up at the stalk. She'd have to climb it, and she would never make it to the motel. The Wild was right. Goldie was right.

Goldie pinched her. "Pay attention. Do you know how to stop the Wild?"

"Ow," Julie said. "Yes. Mom told me . . ."

"Then you're our best hope," Goldie said. She put her hands on the beanstalk leaves. "Rapunzel owes me one. Cindy too. All of them, in fact." She stepped onto the base and started to climb the stalk. "Oh, I can't believe I'm doing this. I could fall. I could meet a giant . . ."

Julie couldn't believe it either. Goldie was sacrificing herself for Julie? No, Goldie was doing it for herself. She wanted out of the Wild, and Julie was her best hope. Julie didn't want to be anyone's best hope. So many people were depending on her, and she was still nearly three miles from the Wishing Well Motel. "Get going, you nitwit!" Goldie called down to her. "Whatever secret Zel told you, use it!"

Julie started to run. Rounding the beanstalk, she raced down the cobblestones past the moss-covered library, past the overgrown Shell station, and past a downed helicopter. Leaving downtown, Julie plunged back into the thick of the woods as Goldilocks climbed high into the clouds.

Chapter Twenty
The Apple

Candy (lemon drops, Swedish fish, gummy bears, and Jolly Ranchers) dotted the roof, crystallized sugar coated the windows, and lollipops lined the shutters. The picnic tables were carved from Hostess cupcakes. Slowing, Julie stared at the candy cane fence and the Mallomar shrubbery of the former Dairy Hut. Without thinking, she licked her lips. She hadn't eaten since—

She felt claws on her ankle. "Yow!"

"You can't stop here," Boots hissed.

Boots? How . . .

"Move! Move! If you stop, the story will start!"

She hurried past the gingerbread house. Had the witch seen them? She glanced back over her shoulder. Smoke curled out of the gumdrop chimney, but the door stayed shut. With no one nibbling, the witch had no cue to come outside.

As soon as the gingerbread house was behind them, Julie bent down and studied Boots. Was it him or the Wild? He didn't seem to have the same puppet stiffness, and his eyes weren't as flat black. He twitched his ears in annoyance. "What? Did I sprout an extra tail or something?"

Certainly sounded like Boots. But how had he found her so fast if the Wild hadn't magicked him here? If the Wild had arranged for her to find Boots with the bikes, how did she know it wasn't arranging this reunion now? "How did you catch up with me?"

He displayed his claws. "Hitched a ride on a mobile pumpkin."

Certainly acted like Boots.

"Quit looking at me like I'm possessed," Boots said. "It's just me."

No way could the Wild imitate that tone. It was pure Boots. Tears popping into her eyes, she scooped him up. "Thought I'd lost you for a minute there. Only have one brother, you know."

He squirmed. "Ack, don't ruffle the fur." She released him, and he leapt to the ground. "Your fault if you'd lost me. You ditched me back there." She heard a note of real hurt in his voice.

She hadn't meant to abandon him, not like he'd left her when he first went into the woods. "You were possessed," she said. Maybe she should feel encouraged that the Wild had talked through Boots. The Wild clearly felt threatened—and that meant they were on the right track.

"Yeah, well, I'm feeling much better now." He licked his fur flat. "Much better." He called into the bushes: "Precious, you can come out."

A cat, a white longhair, emerged from the bushes behind him. The cat was carrying a paper bag in her mouth.

Julie looked from Boots to "Precious" and back again. Had he done it? Had he found himself a girlfriend? Precious sat down and curled her tail around herself. "Hello," the new cat said.

"Precious, this is Julie. Julie, meet the love of my life," Boots said, nuzzling the white cat with his whiskers. "I found her in town while you were talking with Goldie."

Wow, that was . . . fast. Love of his life? She must have been extremely charming to win him in the three minutes that Julie was talking to Goldie. Or was this how love worked in the Wild? Love at first sight is traditional in fairy tales, she thought. And Boots had desperately wanted to find love. The fact that Precious could talk was probably enough to win him.

"Nice to meet you," Julie said. She tried to sound enthusiastic. Boots had finally gotten himself a girlfriend. Everything was working out—she had found Mom, Boots had found his girl-cat, and now they were on their way out of "happily"-ever-after land. "She can come with us," Julie said. "Let's go."

The white cat nudged Boots. "Don't be shy," she said. "You said you wanted to give it to her."

"Give me what?" Julie asked. How much did Boots know about Precious? Could they trust her? What if she was part of a story? Julie had never heard of a story with two talking cats, though.

He cleared his throat. "We brought you lunch."

Oh. That was sweet. But she couldn't stop for lunch. They were almost there! Her stomach rumbled in protest. She hadn't eaten since she'd entered the woods. "We have to reach the motel . . ."

"I just . . . thought you might like it," he said.

She stared at him for a second. Was this an apology? For Boots, food was probably the closest to an apology that she was going to get. "Really bothered you when the Wild took you over, didn't it?"

Dropping his head, he said nothing.

"You don't have to make it up to me," she said.

"I know," he said. And the white cat nosed the paper bag toward Julie's feet.

She couldn't refuse a peace offering from Boots—they were rare. Julie picked up the bag. What if it was candy from the gingerbread house? She shouldn't eat anything from there. She could pretend to eat and then throw it out. Opening the bag, she took out a sandwich and lifted the bread: ham and cheese with mustard. She would have felt safer with PB&J, but it wasn't so bad. At worst, it was one of the Three Little Pigs. She owed Boots an apology for being suspicious. "We can split it," she offered.

"There's more," the white cat said.

"That's okay," Boots said simultaneously. "I don't need any."

Looking for a second sandwich, Julie rooted through the bag: napkins, crackers . . . a Red Delicious apple. Oh, no.

A red apple. In the Wild.

She tried to toss the bag. Instead, her hand pulled out the apple, and the empty bag fell to her feet. "Boots . . ." she said. He flinched as if she'd hit him. Ears flattened, looking miserable, he huddled on the forest floor. Beside him, Precious watched her with an unreadable expression.

Throw it, she told her arm. Drop it! Now! Her muscles wouldn't obey, and her hand lifted the apple to her mouth.

No, no, no! But her mouth opened, and her teeth sank into the apple's red skin. The wet crunch seemed to echo, and she tasted the juice on her tongue.

"Sorry, Julie," Boots whispered. The white cat purred. And everything went black.

*　*　*

Thud. A sudden jolt. Julie hacked—apple bits flew out of her throat.

Air! She needed air! She gasped in and her lungs squeezed. Coughing, she bent up, and her forehead smacked into something solid. She flattened back down.

She opened her eyes, wincing. Warped through glass, she saw blue sky, a smear of leaves, and seven faces pressed against the glass peering down at her. She screamed and recoiled—directly into more glass.

She was enclosed: glass on all sides. She pounded on it. "Let me out!" she shouted. "Let me out of here!" She pushed upward with her hands and her feet.

She heard a click, and the glass coffin opened. She sat up quickly, and the world swam. She squeezed her eyes shut. What happened? Where was she? Gingerly, she felt her head and opened her eyes.

She was surrounded by dwarves.

"Oh, no, not you," she said. She scooted backward. How did she get with *them*? She remembered the apple . . .

Oh, idiot.

"My Snow White," a boy's voice said.

Boots, what have you done? Why did you do it? She thought of the white cat. How convenient that Boots found the one thing he always wanted right when Julie was close to the motel. She'd worried that Precious was part of a story bit, but she hadn't thought about any other kind of trap, a voluntary trap. Had Precious been a bribe or a reward? It was bad enough thinking that the Wild had used her own brother as an unwitting pawn, but to think that Boots had *chosen* to betray her . . .

A boy—fourteen or fifteen with curly black hair—strode across the clearing. "Oh, fair beauty!" he cried. She looked over her shoulder to see if there was someone behind her, someone prettier. But there was only the forest, silent and shadowed.

The dwarves hurried in front of the coffin, in between her and the prince. "Run!" they shouted. "Hurry!" Julie swung one leg over to climb out of the coffin, and the prince pushed through the dwarves as if they were no more than shrubbery in his way.

"Julie!" the dwarves shouted. They do know my name, she thought. "The kiss ends the story! The kiss is an ending! You're about to forget!" they said.

And the prince was in front of her. She was trapped, half in and half out of the coffin. Trees hemmed her in on all sides—had they moved closer? She could no longer see the dwarves, just the prince. He was going to *kiss* her? A zillion scenes from movies flashed through her head. Inches from her, his nose loomed huge. She shouldn't let him kiss her—it would end the story. But she felt frozen; her limbs wouldn't move.

Gently, he placed his lips on hers. Her eyes were wide open—his eyes were so close they blurred into one oblong iris. His lips felt soft and warm. His mouth opened, and she felt his tongue move between her lips. It felt like fried egg in her mouth. She yanked away.

He looked at her and she stared back at him. He'd kissed her. She'd never been kissed before. She wasn't sure she liked it. She wasn't sure she *didn't* like it. She thought she might want to try it again. But he didn't move toward her. He didn't even smile. Had she done it wrong? He opened his mouth to speak, and she didn't breathe. "And they lived happily ever after," he said in a flat voice—as flat as the Wild when it spoke through Boots.

And the woods vanished.

Chapter Twenty-one
In the Tower

Alarmed, Zel watched her hair grow. New hair spilled out of her scalp at a rate of one inch per second. Already she had twelve feet of hair. Coiled on the floor, it looked like a golden boa constrictor. Fresh mounds slid over each other as it grew.

She knew what would happen next: first a witch would come, then a prince. Later, she would be banished to the desert, and the prince would be thrown on briars and blinded. Later still, she would find him and cry on his eyes. And the second her tears touched his eyes, the story would end and she would forget.

She had to make reminders. Quickly. Zel cast about for something, anything, to shape into clues for herself. Bare stone walls. Dirty floor. The Wild knew so many of her tricks. She'd have to be clever if she wanted any chance of leaving a reminder it wouldn't transform.

She'd forgotten so much already, just from living. She could only vaguely remember what Julie's father looked like. He'd had green-blue eyes, like the ocean in New England. His eyes used to crinkle when he smiled. The rest of him was a blur, but she remembered his eyes, and she remembered his hands. His hands could cover hers easily.

She looked at her own smooth, pale hands that hadn't scarred or tanned or aged in five hundred years. Five hundred years. Zel could bear to lose all of those years except the last twelve. She didn't want to forget Julie.

"Rapunzel, Rapunzel, let down your hair to me!"

At the command, Zel yanked at her hair. The coils slid and flopped. She didn't want to forget the day that Julie was born, when she first looked at Julie's pink, scrunched face and felt as if the sun itself had flared up inside her chest.

"Oh, Rapunzel?"

She didn't want to forget Julie's first steps: how she went straight from walk to run to fall. She didn't want to forget the way Julie used to leap into Zel's bed or the way she cleaned her room by throwing everything in the closet or the way she argued with Boots over TV channels.

Compelled by the Wild, Zel leaned out the window. Down below, Gothel waited, broom in hand and black dress billowing in the breeze. "Are you waiting for Christmas?" Gothel called. "Come on, Zel, lower the hair!"

Zel blinked. That was strange. Gothel sounded like herself. She'd never varied from the witch's lines before. "Mom?" she called down. "Are you all right?"

"Just peachy!" Gothel called back.

She was herself! What did it mean? Were things going to be different this time around? With the Wild growing so fast and subsuming so many new people, all the story bits were jumbled up. But did that mean there was truly a chance for change for the Wild's original residents? Did Zel dare hope? "Hair's coming!" Zel shoveled the mounds of hair onto the windowsill. It teetered there, a massive heap. She pushed it over. It tumbled down the tower wall. She braced herself on the window frame as the weight of it pulled her forward.

Gothel grasped it, and Zel's scalp was yanked forward. "Yow!" Another thing she'd forgotten: how much this hurt. "Ow-ow-OW!" It felt as if her head was going to pop off like a Barbie doll's. Gritting her teeth, Zel hung on to the window frame as Gothel climbed the outside wall of the tower.

Zel gasped as Gothel, scrambling over the windowsill, released her hair. Blinking back tears that had popped into her eyes, Zel reeled her hair inside. Sitting down on the puddle of hair, she massaged her scalp.

"I've never understood why I don't just fly up here," Gothel said lightly.

Zel grunted. It was going to be even worse when the

new prince came. Any prince the Wild picked was bound to be heavier than Gothel. It didn't matter if Zel's scalp was strong enough; it still *hurt*. She really hated this.

Gothel was silent for a moment as Zel conquered the pain. When Zel looked up, her mother was staring out the window. "All the years outside and here we are again," Gothel said. "I had hoped that after five hundred years, my role would have changed."

Zel didn't know what to say. Gothel was right: five hundred years out of the Wild, yet Zel was still the girl in the tower and Gothel was still her jailer. "Mother . . ."

Continuing to stare out the window, Gothel said, "I have some news you're not going to like."

Zel felt the bottom drop out of her stomach, and her hair was forgotten. Something had happened to Julie. She knew it. Her baby was hurt, and Zel was unable to go to her. She clenched her fists, wishing she could pummel the walls until they fell. She'd been unable to keep her daughter safe from the Wild. She would never forgive herself. "Tell me," she said.

"Julie's in the woods," Gothel said. "I saw her. She's looking for you."

Zel almost melted into the floor with relief. That was the news? She knew that. "I know. She found me." She must have found Gothel too. She must have been the one who reminded Gothel who she was.

"Good for her," Gothel said, smiling. She looked around the tower room. "Where is she?"

Shaking out her hair, Zel got to her feet and looked out the window. Dark green, the Wild stretched like a smothering blanket to the horizon. "She's on her way to the well," she said.

Gothel's eyebrows shot up into the crinkles of her forehead. "You let her go back out there?"

Zel flared up. "I didn't have a choice! She wasn't safe here." Gothel's silence spoke volumes. "At least out there she has a chance of making it," Zel said. Again, Gothel said nothing. Zel wilted. Be honest, she told herself. It had taken her years of tries to get there. She'd had to reenact her story countless times before she'd succeeded. Julie was only twelve years old. How could she make it? "She doesn't have a chance," she whispered. Oh, what had she done? Sent her only daughter out for the Wild to toy with, that's what she'd done.

Awkwardly, Gothel patted her shoulder. She didn't need to say anything. There wasn't anything she could say.

It's not right, Zel thought. Julie should have the whole wide, wonderful world, not just this sad set of stories. She deserved more than "ever after." She should have every day, new and unique.

For a long while, Rapunzel and the witch stood side by side silently at the window looking out over the green expanse of Wild.

Zel smiled briefly, remembering. "You should have seen her—facing down the Wild. Determination in her eyes. I was so proud of her." The smile faded. "I wish I'd told her that."

"You told her what to wish for if she gets there?" Gothel asked.

Zel nodded. "Her heart's desire."

"She might make it," Gothel said. Zel heard the doubt in her voice.

Chapter Twenty-two
The Mysterious Princess from Unknown Lands

Once upon a time, there was a girl in a forest. . . .

She had a knife at her throat. The blade felt cool, smooth, and flat. A hand held her arm, and she felt breath on the back of her head, warm on her scalp. She looked out at trees. Sunlight came down between the trees in shafts. The forest was green and gold. Except for the heavy breath behind her, it was silent. Not even a leaf moved.

The girl tried to turn her head slightly, and the knife pressed against her windpipe. She wondered if that was a bad thing. Behind her, her captor began to sob. "Forgive me, princess," he said—a deep voice, one she didn't recognize. "The queen's mirror says that you, with your skin as white as snow, are the fairest in the land, and so the queen has commanded me to kill you."

Princess? Queen? *Kill?* She clutched at his knife arm as fear coursed through her so suddenly that she felt dizzy. "Please, don't!"

He released her, and she scrambled away from him. She backed against a tree. She wanted to run, but the same fear held her feet frozen. She rubbed her throat as the man buried his face in his sleeve. "I could never hurt such innocence," he said. "I will kill a deer for the queen and tell her it is your heart she eats instead."

Someone wanted to eat her heart? "Please," she said, "let me run away."

"Run away, then, you poor child," he said. "The wild beasts will soon catch you."

Her legs started moving, almost on their own. Leaves snagged her hair, and she stumbled as her shoes snagged on roots and rocks. Branches curled like claws over her head. Knots and holes leered like faces. She heard beasts roaring, and she kept running and running . . .

Exhausted, she stumbled over a root and sprawled onto the pine-needle-covered ground. Above her, wind moved the trees, and branches seemed to reach for her. Unable to help herself, she started to cry.

"Why are you crying, Girl?" a kind voice said. "Do you wish to go to the ball?" An oak tree made a popping sound. Bark swung open like a door, and light poured out of the trunk. Surprise stopped her tears.

Briefly, she wondered what she was surprised at: the sudden voice or the fact that the tree had a door—but the thought felt unimportant and Girl let it drift away.

Getting to her feet, she stepped cautiously toward the tree and peered inside. Through the opening, she saw a marble hall lined with pillars. She drew back, again feeling surprise. This time, she was sure she was surprised at the tree: it was larger inside than outside. But it was hard to hold on to the feeling of surprise. She supposed this must be how trees were.

Coming around one of the pillars, a woman in a bathing suit and sunglasses waved at her. "Ah, there you are!" The woman bounced toward her, her toes barely touching the floor. "I've been expecting you."

Girl frowned. After two surprises, she now had practice in pinpointing the emotion's source: she was surprised at "expecting you." "How could you be expecting me?" she asked. "I didn't plan to come here. I just ran."

For an instant, the woman faltered, and her smile slipped from her face. Then the smile was back beaming so quickly that Girl thought she must have imagined it. "You can't go to the ball looking like this." The woman tsked. She took Girl's hand and pulled her inside the tree. Butterfly wings fluttered on the woman's back between the straps of the bathing suit. Girl twisted to feel her own back. She was wingless.

The fairy godmother waved her free hand, and a wand popped into the air in front of her. She plucked the wand out of the air and pointed it at a marble pillar. A picture of a golden ball gown appeared on the marble. It sashayed across the face of the pillar. The fairy lifted her sunglasses. "Mmm, no," she said. She pointed at the next pillar, and a silver dress shimmered and curtsied. On the third, a ball gown studded in rhinestone stars spun in a slow circle. On the fourth, a dress composed entirely of feathers descended from the top. Its skirt poofed until its hem touched the base of the pillar. "Yes," the fairy said to the feather dress. "You will do." She waved her wand at the pillar.

Girl felt wind spiral up from her feet. It circled up her legs, up her torso. She lifted her arms in the air, and the wind cycloned over her head, pulling her hair up into a twist, and then it was gone. When she looked down, she was wearing the feather dress.

The fairy clasped her hands. "Perfect as a princess!"

Girl stared at herself. From her neck to her waist, the dress was an intricate pattern of tiny green and gold feathers, each as brilliant as a jewel. From her waist to the floor, she wore sweeping plumes of black, white, and navy. Peacock feathers draped down her arms. "How did you . . . How am I . . ." She touched the feathers, awed. Each one shimmered.

"Don't ask questions," the fairy said. She tapped the marble floor with her wand. A mirror with a crown of leaves sprouted in front of Girl. *"Oh, wondrous beauty that I see,"* the mirror said. *"The fairest of the land stands before me."*

Girl gawked in the mirror. Amazing. She was . . . I'm beautiful, she thought. I look like a . . . like a . . . the phrase "fairy-tale princess" popped into her mind. Yes, that was it. In wonder, she touched her hair, which had been swept into a tumble of curls. The feathers flowed around her as she moved. "Wow," she said out loud.

Taking her arm, the fairy propelled her across the hall toward a blank marble wall. Girl resisted, wanting to look in the mirror longer. At the tap of the wand, a door opened in the marble. "Now, remember: it all changes back at midnight."

"What . . ." Girl began as the fairy godmother guided her through the door. "Down you go," the fairy said, "and have a lovely time!"

She shut the door, and Girl was alone in darkness. "Come back, please," she said. She knocked on the door. What ball? Where was she supposed to go? The questions made her head spin and throb.

Candles flickered to life around her. As the light grew, she saw that she was pounding on a solid wall. The door was gone. She was bewildered. Her head began to pound harder. None of this made sense!

Did it matter that it didn't make sense? she asked herself. She couldn't answer that. With an inward shrug, she gave up on her questions.

Instantly, her head felt better. It was much more pleasant not to question.

She looked around her. Behind her, a staircase descended into shadows. *Down you go*, the fairy had said. Lifting the skirt of her feather dress, Girl started down the stairs. Her shoes clinked with each step. Stopping, she raised her skirt higher to peer over the feathers at her feet. She was wearing glass shoes instead of bright yellow sandals. They must have changed with the clothes. She twisted her feet, admiring them. They sparkled with the amber light of the candle flames.

At the end of the staircase, she found herself in a forest of silver. Wide-eyed, she looked around her. The trees shimmered—the leaves and bark were solid sterling. Gone was the daylight of the huntsman's forest. A fat, silver moon hung low in the leaves and bathed her and this forest in a pale light. It was beautiful. She'd never seen anything so beautiful. Had she? She reached for a memory, but it felt like trying to catch air. She abandoned the effort.

She started walking down a smooth, white path. Silence wrapped around her. Even her steps were muffled. Soon, the silver woods gave way to trees of gold, then to trees all of diamond. She followed the path to the shore of a blue-black lake. The fat moon hovered over the horizon. Staring at the water, she felt déjà vu, as if she'd once looked across water like this, but no memory came, so she ignored the feeling. In a swath of moonlight, a flower-decked rowboat drifted toward the shore.

As the boat came closer, she saw it was empty. Slowing, it stopped in front of her. It stayed there, as if waiting. Was it waiting for her? Girl looked to either side of her, but she saw no one. She looked back at the boat, patient in the water. Wondering if she should be worried, she stepped into the boat.

The boat rocked underneath her as she sat at its helm. Leaning forward, she searched for oars. A wave tilted her toward the water, and she looked up. Without oars or sails, the boat was moving unerringly down the path of moonlight. She heard the sound of a trumpet.

Ahead of her, rising over the horizon beneath the moon, she saw an island castle, lit with candles along the battlements. Laughter and trumpet music floated across the water. In the distance, slow waterfalls seeped down mountainsides. "Tears of unhappy lovers," a voice said behind her.

She turned quickly, and at the back of the boat, she saw the silhouette of a gondolier. With a black stick, he propelled the boat through the moonlight. She couldn't see his face. "Who are you?" she asked.

But he only hummed to himself, jarring with the trumpet solo from the castle. Girl shivered. It disturbed her that he hadn't answered. He had to have a name. Didn't he? Looking across the moonlight, she saw another boat. Two rounded people sat facing each other. Who were they? Did they have names? As they drew closer, she saw they weren't people at all. An owl strummed a guitar. A cat with a parasol sat opposite him. Behind the gondola, the shore disappeared in darkness.

She felt a bump as the gondolier pulled the boat into a candlelit dock. He gestured to the castle. Pale marble, the castle matched the moon's glow. Spires stretched into the night sky. Roses and ivy wound halfway up their sides. A servant, face blank and shadowed like the gondolier's, stood on the dock. He held his hand out to her. How elegant, she thought. Smiling, she took his hand and let him help her out of the boat. She followed him down the dock to shore. When she reached the foot of the castle, she looked back over her shoulder, but the flowered boat and its gondolier were gone. The owl and the pussycat drifted over the waves.

The servant led her through an archway (WHITE CLIFFS RESTAURANT, she read on the arch) into an ornate hall. She craned her neck at tapestries on the walls, but they were so high and dimly lit that she saw only swirled colors and an occasional human or animal face caught in an almost-scream.

The hall opened onto a balcony. Bowing, the servant left her there, and she walked forward. She was at the top of a spiral staircase that led down into a vast ballroom. Chandeliers with a thousand candles glittered from the ceiling. Mirrors, three stories high, decorated the walls between ivory pillars.

Below was the ball.

A single trumpet played. Laughing, lords and ladies and bears and lions and trolls swirled in a dance as colorful as a kaleidoscope. Silver and gold gowns sparkled in the candlelight, reflected countless times in the mirrors.

"My lady," a footman said, "I must announce you. What is your name?"

She opened her mouth to speak, and no name came out. Her name . . . She pressed her hands to her forehead and tried to think. Who was she? What was her name? "I don't know," she whispered. "I don't remember."

She remembered the huntsman. She remembered the knife at her throat. But what came before the huntsman? Something had to have come before the huntsman. She had to have been *somewhere* before she was there. She hadn't been born there in the woods with the huntsman and the knife. Had she? Of course not. She felt panic bubble up in her throat. The farthest back she could remember was the huntsman—the huntsman who called her "princess." She clutched the footman's arm. "Princess," she said.

The footman bellowed, "The mysterious princess from unknown lands!" She felt a surge of relief. She knew who she was now. For some reason that she couldn't name, it had bothered her immensely not to know. Now everything was all right. She was Princess.

The lords and ladies halted their dance. In unison, their faces turned toward Princess. Oddly, the trumpet kept playing, and the bears and lions and wild boars kept dancing.

The lords and ladies began to whisper: *"Beautiful." "Exquisite." "Who is she?" "Princess."* The words rose up to the balcony, and she felt herself start to smile. Instinctively, as if the whispers were a command, she laid her hand on the stair railing. The ivory stairs curved down to an inlaid marble floor. Slowly, just like a princess, she descended the grand spiral staircase. The lords and ladies watched her. Someone sighed adoringly. She straightened her posture. All those eyes, all on her! She felt as if she were floating.

At the bottom of the stairs, the lords and ladies pressed toward her. One tentatively reached out and touched her feather dress. "Ooh," the lady said, and the circle tightened. Shoulder to shoulder, they stared at her. Princess started to feel uneasy. It was nice and flattering, but now they were a little close . . . A lion began to growl as the trumpet soloist faltered.

Red Sea-like, the lords and ladies parted. A sandy-haired boy wearing a crown and ballet tights strode between them. In front of Princess, he dropped to one knee and bowed his head. "Would you do me the honor of granting me this dance?"

Before she could answer, the prince took her hand. He led her to the center of the floor, and the lords and ladies parted into a wide arc. The trumpet music resumed, and lions pranced around them. She thought she saw a unicorn.

"You dance like an angel," he said, and took a sweeping step to the left. Her dress caught around her ankles, and she wobbled on the glass slippers. Feathers stabbed into her waist as she stumbled. He held her upright and swept her across the dance floor. All the other dancers clapped in odd unison.

The prince whispered in her ear, "You are the most beautiful sight I have ever seen." His breath was warm on her cheek. She felt herself flush. A prince thought she was beautiful. Of course he did. She had seen herself: she was the beautiful princess.

Chapter Twenty-three
The Princess Test

The trumpet stopped suddenly.

Mid-step, the prince stumbled. Princess looked around, confused, as spinning dancers slowed like a dying music box. Around her, the lions and bears snarled and growled. She wondered if she should be alarmed.

"*I found you!*" a voice rang out across the ballroom. Princess saw the trumpet player—a girl—wave. She seemed to be waving at Princess. Or perhaps at the prince. The prince put his arm protectively around Princess.

The trumpet player lifted her trumpet to her lips and played a flourish, and the lions, trolls, and bears began to dance again. Laughing, the lords and ladies swirled, and the trumpet player walked through them. "Knew if I played"—she trilled notes—"long enough"—more notes—"it would draw you."

In a wave, a stream of rats flowed after the musician. In

their wake came a flood of laughing, dancing children. The prince began to draw Princess backward, away from the odd procession.

"Did you find"—the trumpet girl played another set of notes, then finished the sentence—"your mom?" More notes. "Do you know how to stop the Wild?"

Princess frowned.

"I want"—more notes—"to go home." Flourish of notes up the scale and down. She took a breath. "I've had enough adventure."

Home? Mom? Adventure? Wild? Princess felt as if small fireworks were popping inside her head with each word. And with each pop came a flood of questions: who was the trumpet girl? How did she know Princess? What did she mean, adventure? What did she mean, "stop the Wild"? What was "the Wild"? What was home?

She opened her mouth to let the questions pour out, but the prince pulled her away. Quickly, the lords and ladies spun in dancing couples between them and the trumpet girl, as if attempting to deliberately part them. The river of rats and children clogged the open spaces. Princess wanted to cry: Wait! Who are you? But the prince was herding her too quickly back toward the ivory staircase.

A woman in red velvet descended the staircase.

"Mother!" the prince cried. "This is the Mysterious Princess from Unknown Lands. She is the one I love."

Love? He loved her? It was as if the trumpet girl had released a dam. More questions tumbled into Princess's swirling mind: How could he love her? He barely knew her. She barely knew him. She barely knew herself.

"Indeed," said his mother, the queen. "Your brother said the same about the girl from the last midnight, and she was little more than a scullery maid with high-quality shoes, when all was said and done." She fixed her gaze on Princess, and Princess felt like wilting. "Are you a true princess?"

Was she? She didn't know. If she wasn't a princess, what was she? This time, when Princess reached back for a memory, it felt as if she slammed into a wall inside her head.

The prince clasped Princess's hand to his heart. "Surely she is a princess from some faraway land. Look at her grace, her beauty, her poise!"

"We shall see," the queen said. "She shall be tested."

* * *

Leaving the prince behind, the queen shepherded Princess down a tapestry-lined hall. Questions tumbled inside her: What test? Why? Who was this queen? Where was this castle? The queen pulled her faster and faster down the hall until the tapestries blurred into a mosaic of colors, and the glass slippers echoed and clinked like a dozen champagne flutes toasting.

Abruptly, the queen halted and flung open a door. The

scent of roses flowed out like a wave, and Princess saw a blond woman in a pink ball gown sleeping peacefully on a canopied bed. Roses climbed up the posts and over the canopy. "Who is she?" Princess asked.

"Occupied," the queen said. "Not your story. Come. We must find your story." She took Princess by the wrist again and hurried down the hall. What did she mean? Princess wondered. Her story?

Again without warning, the queen halted. Sliding on her glass slippers, Princess narrowly avoided crashing into the queen. The queen threw open another door. Princess peeked inside. In front of a mountain of straw, a girl was crying. "Is she all right? Why is she crying?" Princess started to ask, but the queen slammed the door shut and pulled Princess onward. "There must be a role for you," the queen muttered. "You must fit one of them."

Princess didn't know what she meant. Her feet ached in the hard shoes, and her skin itched from the feathers. Who were these people? What was she doing here? "Please, can't we rest?" she asked, but the queen ignored her.

The queen tried a third door, where an older woman studied herself in a mirror and chanted: *"Mirror, mirror, on the wall . . ."* The next room had another bed, but this time, it housed a woman and a fat, green frog. "Who are they?" Princess asked.

"You should not be asking," the queen said flatly. "The

trumpeter will be punished for this."

"But I . . ."

The queen opened another door. "Ah," the queen said. "Here we are, and in you go." She shooed Princess through the doorway.

Princess faced a wall of cloth. She craned her neck. Mattresses, she realized. It was a pile of mattresses. Lots of mattresses. Why were there so many? The stack peaked near the top of the vaulted ceiling, twenty feet overhead. A ladder leaned against it. Princess heard a bolt slide into a lock behind her. She heard the queen's voice through the shut door: "Sleep well."

Sleep? The queen was leaving her here? "Wait, please." Princess tried the door handle. It didn't budge. She knocked. "I don't understand! You said there would be a test."

Behind her, within the room, a voice said, "This *is* the test."

She turned and saw only the mattresses. "Who said that?"

"I did," the voice said.

She looked up. Poking its head over the top mattress was a cat. "Hello," she said. "What do you mean, it's the test?"

"The queen has placed a pea under the mattresses that a true princess would feel while she slept," he said.

She didn't think that sounded very likely. The ladder to the top was so long that it bowed in the middle. "A pea?"

"It's an unusually large pea," he said.

What did a pea have to do with being a princess? How could a vegetable confirm an identity?

The cat disappeared for a moment and then reappeared to climb, humanlike, down the ladder. He wore boots on his hind paws, and he had a tan-colored cloak tied around his neck in place of a collar. A stick poked out of one of his boots. She wondered if it was normal for a cat to talk and wear clothes. It felt odd and familiar at the same time, as if a memory should be there, but of course it wasn't. He landed neatly on the ground and stood upright on his booted hind paws. "Why does a cat need boots?" she asked. "And why wear them only on your back feet?"

His whiskers twitched. "You're too aware," he said. "You shouldn't be asking so many questions."

"Why not?" What was wrong with being aware? She didn't feel particularly aware. She felt as if she were swimming in murk. She tried again to push at her memories, and she hit the wall in her head. Her head throbbed.

"You must have found a reminder," he said. "Something or someone must have sparked this." He hesitated and then asked, "Do you know who I am?"

She frowned, thinking of the trumpet girl—that was when the questions had begun to flow. The trumpet girl had sparked this feeling of . . . She didn't know how to name this feeling. Absently, Princess plucked at the feathers on her sleeve. The peacock feathers tickled her arms, and the shafts poked her skin. It itched. "Maybe," she said. "I don't know." She half felt as if she did know him, and she half felt as if she didn't.

"Oh, this is not good," he said. "Not good at all."

She scratched her arms through the feathers and had a flash of memory: soft hands rubbing calamine lotion on her arms because she had followed a cat—this cat!—into a field of poison ivy. Excitement bubbled up. A memory! A real memory! "I *do* know you. Don't I?"

The cat flinched as if she had hit him.

There *were* memories beyond that wall. Gritting her teeth, she tried to push. If she battered at it long enough, would there be a point where the wall broke?

"You must climb into bed," the cat said. He sounded oddly desperate. "If you don't and you fail the test, the queen will kill you."

Her memories scattered. "*Kill* me?"

"It's the rules," he said.

"But . . ." she began as a dozen questions rushed into her head.

"Please, climb," he begged.

He sounded so insistent that she obeyed without thinking. The ladder bent and swayed under her weight. At the top, she found a nightgown. How did it get here? Was it for her? She leaned over the edge to ask the cat. He was curled on the floor as if asleep. "Cat? Hello? Are you awake?"

He didn't answer. She sat for a moment, alone with her questions, and then she squirmed out of the itchy feather dress and into the soft nightgown. She kicked the feather dress to the bottom of the bed and lay down.

She closed her eyes, but she didn't think she'd fall asleep.

*   *   *

She had to find . . . what? The dream was gone. She blinked around her at the ornate ceiling. She was on the mattress stack, she remembered. She hadn't felt any pea.

Guess I'm not a princess, she thought.

Now that she was fully awake, her breath tasted stale and she needed to pee. Girl climbed down the ladder.

Stepping over the sleeping cat, she found a door on the other side of the mattress stack. She hadn't remembered it being there before she slept, but it led to a closet-sized bathroom with a marble sink and toilet. She rinsed her mouth. "Boots, have you seen my toothbrush?" She studied herself in the mirror.

The cat ran into the bathroom. "Julie?"

Her hair was matted on the left side. She tried to fluff it out. Obviously, she wasn't a princess. Princesses didn't have bad-hair days. "Sorry—what did you say?"

He sank down to four paws. "I didn't think it would be so bad to see you like this," he said. "I'm a cat; you're a girl—why do I care?"

"What's so bad?" she asked. Her hair? She wished the fairy godmother hadn't coiled her hair. It might have looked exotic at the ball, but not anymore. She had serious un-princesslike bed head. Whoever she was, she was definitely not a princess.

"You remembered my name," he said.

Hands in her hair, she froze. Yes, she had remembered: Boots. His name was Puss-in-Boots. She had reached for the name, and there it was. She hadn't even realized she'd done it. "I know you," she said. "How do I know you? How do you know me?" He retreated out of the bathroom, and she followed him. "You said a name. What was the name? Who am I?"

The bolt slid on the bedroom door, and she heard the queen's voice singsong: "Oh, love-ly prin-cess?" Girl knelt down on the floor in front of Boots and begged, "Quickly, please. Tell me! Tell me who I am!"

"If I do, I'll lose her!" Boots said.

"Who?" she whispered back.

"The love of my life!" he said. "It was the bargain . . ."

The queen came around the mattresses. "Ah, there you are! How did you sleep?"

Girl straightened. "I wasn't able to sleep, Your

Majesty," she found herself saying. "There was an awful lump in the bed." Why had she said that? She hadn't meant to say that. It wasn't even true.

The queen clapped. "Marvelous! You are a true princess! You must come now. We will celebrate with a feast."

She was so close to breaking through! She searched for an excuse to stay: "But I'm not dressed." It was true: she was barefoot and in the nightgown.

"Pshaw, you would be radiant in a scullery maid's dress." Putting her arm around her, the queen guided her toward the door. Girl looked back over her shoulder. To her relief, the cat trotted behind her.

The queen hurried her through the ornate halls into a vast dining room. Girl had a quick glimpse: six chandeliers lit the cathedral-shaped hall. Tapestries and mosaics filled the marble walls. At one end, Girl saw a two-story grandfather clock.

"Sit, sit," the queen said. Obeying, Girl climbed onto a throne at one end of a banquet table. Her toes barely touched the floor. She wondered how it could be dinnertime. Shouldn't it be morning? Had she slept through the day? Or had she only slept an hour or two and it was still night? Neither choice felt right. It had felt like morning when she woke. She tried to see around the pyramid of melon slices in front of her. The prince sat at the other end behind sculptures made of bread and pastry. "Here is the true princess!" he shouted. "She has passed the test! She is worthy to be my wife!"

Girl stared. "Wife?"

Smoke billowed from the center of the table. Spilling fruit platters, a boy solidified in the midst of the smoke. He swished midnight blue robes as he strode across the table toward Girl. "No, I forbid it!"

"Where did he come from?" Girl hissed to the cat. "Who is he? Do I know him?" But the cat was no longer in sight. "Boots? Where are you, Boots?" The magician grabbed Girl's wrist and hauled her to her feet. "Ow, hey!" she said.

"She is *my* beloved," the magician said. "I will have her!"

The prince climbed onto the table. "I challenge you to a contest for her love! For I am an enchanter, and I have magic at my disposal!"

Girl tried to twist out of the magician's grip. "Let go."

"Very well, prince," the magician said, releasing her. Girl fell back into the throne. "What are your terms?" he said.

Rubbing her sore wrist, Girl stood up. "Wait a minute here. Don't I have a say?" She was not marrying anybody. She barely knew the prince. She barely knew herself. And who was the kid in the wizard hat? The hat had a tag dangling in the boy's face.

The prince puffed out his chest. "We shall have a

magical duel. Whoever creates the thing that pleases the princess most shall have her for his bride."

Magical duel? With her as the prize? She didn't want to be a prize. She didn't want this pimple-faced magician as her husband. She wasn't even sure she wanted the cute prince. What she wanted was her name. She headed for the door. "Boots? Boots!"

The prince pushed his royal sleeves to his royal elbows and said, "I shall begin, since I was first to claim her hand." He waved his arms in the air. "I summon the birds of the sky!"

As Girl reached the door, it slammed open in front of her. Birds flooded into the hall. Covering her head, she ran back to the banquet table as dozens of parrots dive-bombed her shoulders. She stooped under the table.

The birds dove around the hall chirping: "Beautiful, beautiful princess. Beautiful, beautiful princess," until the echoes shook the chandeliers.

Cautiously, she peeked out. Green and red parrots swooped in figure eights.

"Ha!" the magician said. "You call that magic? Come, singers of the slime, dwellers of the mud! I summon you!" He waved his arms, and frogs poured through the windows. Hundreds of frogs piled onto the floor and hopped across the banquet hall. She jumped out from under the table and climbed on top of her chair.

Conducting them, the magician led their croaking as he bellowed out aria style: "Admirable princess, do you think it kind or wise, in this sudden way to kill a poor magician with your eyes?" The frog bellows reverberated like an orchestra of bass drums.

"Honestly, I don't . . ." Girl started to say.

But it wasn't over. Wading through the frogs, the prince-enchanter stabbed the wall with a butter knife. It sprang a leak. Soon, cracks spread across the wall, and water poured through onto the floor. Frogs hopped right and left and the birds flew toward the ceiling as the waterfalls engulfed the walls.

Okay, this was not fun. Even the queen lifted her skirts as the water level rose in the hall. Girl climbed onto the table beside the cheese.

At the prince's command, barges came through the wall on either side of the grandfather clock. One by one, the boats squeezed narrow to fit through the cracks, then popped out into their full size. The barges drifted beside the banquet table.

Lying on one of the barges, a woman with seashells in her hair leaned over toward Girl. In place of legs, the woman had a long fish tail with shimmering scales. She handed Girl a pearl and said, "You are even more beautiful than I."

"That's nice," Girl said, "but I don't want this." She

tried to hand the pearl back, but the mermaid floated out of the hall.

Scowling fiercely, the magician blew on a pipe. In response, the river around them bubbled and swirled, turning brown with mud.

Hundreds of thousands of great oysters waddled slowly and laboriously onto the table toward Girl. She scooted to the center of the table as the shells flopped across the plates. "Seriously, you can stop now," she said. "I'm not playing." Row by row, the oysters opened up their shells and each spat a pearl at her feet.

"Princess!" the prince shouted. "Look at this!" He gestured toward the ceiling, and all the birds swooped down, dancing in spirals and twirls like magnificent acrobats.

"No, Princess, look at me!" the magician said. As the candles on the chandeliers detached and danced with the birds, the magician pointed at the muddy river. The water erupted. It shot toward the ceiling and burst through the plaster. Sunlight streamed through as the ceiling shattered and the palace dissolved around them.

Chapter Twenty-Four
Midnight

Only the grandfather clock remained standing. All the castle walls were rubble. Screaming at each other, the prince threw feathers at the magician and the magician hurled frogs at the prince. The hands on the clock clicked: 2:55.

Rain fell on her face as she looked up at the clock. The time made no sense—it was night for the ball, morning when she woke, evening for the feast, and now afternoon? When was midnight? Shouldn't she get a midnight? She had to be home by midnight, the fairy godmother had said. She wanted to go home. She didn't want any more princes or magicians or mattresses or tests. If the clock struck midnight, would she learn where home was?

Climbing off the table, she waded through the water toward the clock. Boots shouted, "Don't do it! Please!" Girl turned to see the cat race across the table and stop short of leaping into the water after her. "If you stop the Wild," Boots said, "I'll lose the love of my life." Behind him, a white cat daintily ate from the feast.

Girl frowned. "What are you talking about?"

He hurried over to the other cat. "Isn't she beautiful? Stylish and intelligent. She's perfect for me, and the Wild said I could have her if you stay in your happily ever after." Girl frowned at him. He wasn't making sense. She turned back to the clock. Desperation in his voice, he said, "You of all people should know how hard it is to be one of a kind, how lonely it is to not belong. I have had this loneliness for hundreds of years, and the Wild offered me a chance to end it. Please, can't you just be happy with this? Can't this be your story?"

The words *not belong* lodged in her head. "I don't belong here?" The words tasted true. She tried them again: "I don't belong here."

The queen slogged through the water toward her. "Nonsense," she said flatly. "You are the princess, on the verge of your happily ever after. Isn't that what you have always wanted? Isn't this the right role for you?"

"I don't know what I've always wanted," she said sharply. "I don't know who I am." She turned to the cat. "But *you* do. Did I want to be a princess?"

"Yes," Boots said, sinking back against the other cat. "Maybe."

"I did?" On the other side of the table, the prince and the magician had drawn swords. Fiercely intent, they swung the swords in elaborate swooping arcs. The blades hissed through the air, missing each other by several feet—which ruined most of the effect of their fierce intent.

"Among other things," Boots added, so quietly that she almost didn't hear him.

"Other things," Girl repeated. "Tell me about the other things."

The queen expanded her arms. "All you ever wanted is here," she said. "Here you are admired and adored. Here you have servants to wait on your every whim. Balls to entertain you. Feasts to fill you. Room after room to call your own."

"But not home," she said. The trumpet player had spoken of home. She'd asked about her mother—had she found her? Girl didn't know. Who was her mother? "What about my family? Where are they? I belong with them." Marching to the clock, she felt along the sides for handholds. The wood was smooth, vertical two stories up to the clock face.

"You don't remember them. You don't even know them to miss them." Continuing in a curiously flat tone, the queen said, "Why can't you be content with what I can give you? Why should your lost past matter?"

The pendulum swayed in front of her. "It matters," Girl said, not turning from the clock. "Family matters." It had mattered to the trumpet player. "Who is my mother?" she asked. "Who's my father? Do I have any brothers or sisters?"

Boots made a sound, half a meow and half a moan.

"Your mother is gone. Your father is gone. And you had no brothers or sisters," the queen said.

"Except for me," Boots said.

Both Girl and the queen turned. Even the white cat stopped eating to stare at him. He hung his head miserably. "You made me your brother," he said. "Even when I abandoned you to enter the woods, you still called me brother."

"A cat cannot be a brother. A cat is a companion," the queen—the Wild—said. "I do not understand this."

"You couldn't," Boots said to the Wild. To the white cat, he said, "I'm sorry, Precious, you're everything I was searching for, but Julie's right—I belong with my family. I wasn't meant to be the villain; I *want* to be the brother." He leapt off the table into the water. He meowed loudly as the water soaked his fur. For an instant, it looked as if he would leap out again, but then he flattened his ears and ran forward. Splashing across the floor, he bounded across the tops of toads and oysters toward the clock. Girl stepped aside. He shed his boots. Claws gouging the ornate wood, he scrambled up the clock. Perching on the rim of the face, Boots swatted at the hands.

Bong!

Water soaked her sandaled feet. She again wore jeans and a sweater. The key to the linen closet again was tucked in her front jeans pocket.

Bong!

Behind her, the queen shrieked. "No! I will not allow this!"

Bong!

"Stop her!" the queen shouted. Dishes rose up from the table and rolled past her. Spoons hopped beside them. They plunged off the table's edge into the water.

Bong!

Three mice with canes ran into the hall and splashed into the shallows. A woman with a meat cleaver chased them. A hedgehog riding on a rooster raced behind them. "Find her a role!" the queen shouted.

Bong!

A shoe fell from the sky and landed in the prince's hand. "I will marry the woman whose foot fits this slipper!" He held it over his head, and birds swooped low over it. The shoe overflowed with blood that ran down the prince's arm as he advanced toward her. She retreated. What was happening? What was . . .

Bong!

A giant ogre echoed in the distance: "Fee, fie, foe, fum . . ."

Bong!

She remembered the ogre. She remembered the magician. She remembered the Wild. She remembered the trumpet player: her best friend, Gillian, who had sparked her memory at the ball. And she remembered herself. "Julie," she said. "My name is Julie."

Bong!

She could have been a princess with a palace and a prince and feasts and balls . . .

"Capture her!" the queen shouted. "Punish her! Stop her! Seize her!"

Julie saw torches and knives waved over cowled heads— a mob that surfaced out of the water. Splashing, she backed against the table as the mob spun into a circle. "Princess impersonator!" they shouted. "False princess! Villain!"

Bong!

"You shall dance in red-hot shoes!" the mob shouted. "You shall be put in a barrel with sharp nails and dragged up the street!"

Bong!

Circling, they brandished their torches. "You shall become a black poodle and have a gold collar around your neck and shall eat burning coals 'til the flames burst forth from your throat!"

Bong!

One woman rose on the backs of salamanders. She leveled a scepter at Julie. "You will prick your finger on the spindle of a spinning wheel . . ."

Bong!

Midnight.

From the top of the clock, Puss-in-Boots yowled, "Julie, catch!" Pulling the ogre's wand out of his boot with his teeth, he tossed it. It spun through the air. "Save our mother! Save Rapunzel! Run, Julie, run!" He was abruptly silent; the Wild must have seized his throat.

Splashing through the water, she ran for the wand. Torches dipped toward her as hands reached for her. She snatched the ogre's wand out of the water. "From a girl to a fish!" She and the wand fell through the air. Belly-flopping into the water, she sank into the dark blue-green.

The wand! Where was the wand? She saw it, suspended in the murk. Wiggling her fin, she dove for it. Opening her fish lips, she aimed for the sinking stick. The wand hit her lips. She closed them firmly over it and kept wiggling. Zigzagging, she wove between human and animal legs.

On the other side of the lake, she flopped onto the shore. She spat out the wand and rolled on top of it. "From a fish to a girl!" Immediately, she morphed back into a girl.

She picked up the wand. She ran through the diamond forest, then the gold, then the silver. Behind her, she heard a thud—thud—thud. She looked over her shoulder as a giant lunged for her. She slapped his fingers with the wand. "Giant to rabbit!"

He shrank and fell behind.

Shrieking, a battalion of witches flew toward her. Touching the tips of their broomsticks, she turned them into birds. Trolls, ogres, and seven-headed dragons—the magic from her wand flew—became frogs, mice, and stone.

The woods closed around her. Branches reached for her as the trees thickened. Bark morphed into walls, trapping her. No! No more woods!

Spinning in a circle, she slapped the branches with the wand and shouted, "From trees to flowers!" The woods around her turned into a meadow. All was suddenly silent.

Julie saw a hunched figure ahead, sitting on a rock in the middle of the meadow. Cautiously, she walked forward. Hooded, the old woman poked at the grasses with the butt of her broomstick. She didn't look up as Julie approached. "Grandma?" Julie said. She stopped a few feet in front of her.

The witch raised her head. With her rheumy red eyes, she regarded Julie. "You have won," the Wild said through her. "I will give you your wish—I will give you your heart's desire."

Home. She'd won. Julie closed her eyes and tried to feel happy. Instead, she felt drained and tired. She remembered everything now: Mom and Boots and Gillian and Kristen and the dwarves and the swan soldiers. She remembered the police and the media and the awfulness that awaited their emergence from the Wild.

Standing creakily, the witch touched the rocks in the meadow with the bristles of her broom. The rocks rose into the air as if lifted by invisible giants. Sailing over the dun-colored grass, the rocks collided. Sticking together, they bubbled into more rocks. The wall grew, budding, down into the earth. Spires spun out of the base. Roses spread across the stones, and flowering trees sprouted around it. An arch widened, and steps carved themselves out of the air. Red cloth rolled down the stairs and across the grass to stop at Julie's feet. A door peeled open at the top, and the castle waited.

Climbing the stairs, Julie went inside.

Sunlight streamed through unfinished holes as the roof of the castle laced itself shut. Chandeliers flew to the ceiling. Ivory silks draped themselves over the walls. Candles burst into flame. Golden statues stepped into alcoves. Marble tiles laid themselves over the floor. Julie walked through the hall as the red carpet knit itself in front of her.

The carpet ran into a throne room and up to a dais enclosed by a curtain. Julie walked up wide marble steps.

She touched the velvet curtain. Of its own accord, it swept open. Golden ropes tied it back on either side of the dais.

On the throne, a man sat as still as stone.

Velvet robes, silk blouse, golden circlet on his head, he looked like a prince. He had pale lines—half-faded scars—on his face, as if he had been scratched, as if he had fallen into a nest of thorns . . . as if he had fallen from a tower into a nest of thorns. *I will give you your heart's desire*, she remembered the Wild had said—and she knew then, without a shadow of a doubt, who he was. He had a cloth wrapped around his eyes. Gently, Julie untied the cloth. It fell into her hands.

He blinked his eyes open. "Rapunzel?"

"Hello, Dad," Julie said.

Chapter Twenty-Five
Heart's Desire

Every year, she had decorated her school locker with illustrations of him. On multiple weekends, she had combed every bookstore and library for hints of him. Many times, she had pretended other fathers were hers, trying to imagine what he would have been like.

None of that had prepared her for this moment.

She felt as if she were standing above Niagara Falls, dizzy with the crashing water. The stuff rolling inside her felt too big, too strong, too scary. She concentrated on the little things: his eyes, his hair, his nose, his mouth. She had his chin and cheekbones. She had his cheeks, though hers were softer and rounded. She wondered if that meant they had the same smile.

"I am 'Dad'?" His voice was softer than she had imagined. Gillian's father's voice boomed across Crawford Street, but her father's didn't penetrate the tapestries. "You are Rapunzel's daughter?"

"Yes," she said—and felt as if she had stepped over the falls. Yes. Yes, she was Rapunzel's daughter. Yes, she was *his* daughter.

She saw emotions flicker across his face so fast that she couldn't read them—did he feel like she did? Was he happy to see her? Oh, what if he wasn't? Maybe he didn't want a daughter. Maybe he didn't want her. He *had* to want her. She was strong enough to survive the woods, beautiful enough to be a princess, and smart enough to outwit the Wild. She was good enough to be his daughter!

"You are grown," he said at last.

Was he disappointed? She felt her heart plummet. "I'm sorry."

"It is all right," he said. She shook with relief. "But . . ." he said, and then hesitated. She lived and died a dozen deaths in that pause. "But it has been *years?*"

"Five hundred years," Julie said.

His face paled and then flushed—thorn scars starkly visible on his cheeks. He hadn't known, she realized. Oh, no. She should have thought to cushion the blow. "I'm sorry!" She was making mistakes right and left. She was ruining this!

He took a deep, raking breath, and his face settled back into its calm, soft look. He took her hand. "Be easy," he said. "It is all right." And suddenly, it was all right. Julie stared at his hand—at *her father's* hand. His hand swallowed hers completely. His palm felt dry, like warm wood.

He said lightly, "You do not look like a five-hundred-year-old."

"I'm twelve," Julie said. "Grandma worked a spell so I wouldn't be born until Mom felt safe."

"'Grandma.' Do you mean Rapunzel's witch?"

"She's not a witch anymore," Julie said. "She's nice. Or at least she was."

"Ahh . . ." He had a faraway look on his face.

What was he thinking? she wondered. She hadn't expected she would feel this . . . this uncertain. She had imagined she would fling herself into his arms. She'd thought she would feel an instant bond. Instead, she couldn't read him.

His eyes swept across the throne room with its ivory buntings, marble walls, and golden statues. "It is different," he said. "Always before, after we reached the end, I woke riding through the woods; you were not here, and I could not remember."

"What do you remember now?" she asked. Maybe if he would tell her, maybe if she could understand what happened, maybe then, the years wouldn't matter.

He closed his eyes. "I remember despair."

"Despair?" she asked, startled.

"We failed," he said softly. "So many times, we failed. After the battle . . . even Rapunzel despaired."

This wasn't what she expected to hear. What about Rapunzel, the valiant rebel? What about Rapunzel, unafraid, like a general? "What else do you remember?"

"Hope." He opened his eyes. "It was the dwarves who gave us hope after all was lost. It would have been over if not for them."

Snow's seven? Snow's seven were useful? She felt guilty as soon as she had the thought—they had tried to keep the prince from kissing her in the glass coffin.

"The dwarves told us of the wishing well," he said. "They risked much to learn its location and to send us word. Risked much and lost much—there were, at the start, thirteen dwarves."

Thirteen? Did he mean . . . ? Were they . . . ? Six *dead*? Julie swallowed hard. Was that why Mom felt she owed them? "So you made a wish?" Was that how Mom and her friends had escaped? It made sense: a wish to make the Wild strong, a wish to make it weak. But if that was true, why hadn't Dad escaped?

"Not I," he said. "It had to be the right wish. Rapunzel in the tower, who could want freedom more than she? Of all of us, she was the one who remembered first, the one who fought the hardest, the one who led the way. She did not know, not for certain, that anything existed beyond the Wild. None of us did. But she never wavered. She believed so strongly in her dream of freedom that she inspired us all." His eyes shone with the memory. "Do you know of her deeds?"

"Bits and pieces," Julie said. "Not the whole story."

"She was our light," he said. "Our beacon in the tower. She was amazing. Cycle after cycle, she would reawaken us and stoke the fires of rebellion. Our rebellions were small at first, but then she conceived the idea of the Great Battle. And she began to prepare us. Painstakingly slowly, so the Wild would not suspect, she laid traps: a woodcutter's ax next to a future beanstalk garden, extra ice to make all the bears' porridge too cold, signposts to replace the bread crumbs so that Hansel and Gretel could find their way home. She drilled us all in our tasks: we were at the same moment to stop every story from continuing. Break glass slippers, protect the Beast's rose, dull the spindles on the spinning wheels, steal all the apples. The Wild rose up against us—every character that Rapunzel could not convert, the Wild used against us, until every ally we had won either perished or fell prey to stories and became our enemy."

Julie could picture it—the reminders that Gothel had told her about, the chaos that the griffin had described, the training the ogre had mentioned . . .

"Rapunzel was the last of us to fall," he said. "Gothel herself trapped Rapunzel in her story by chopping her hair with the same ax that Rapunzel had used on the beanstalk to save Jack. After that, even she despaired, until the dwarves brought their news. It was then she decided that no one else would suffer. She and I alone would continue the fight."

Watching him, Julie saw her mother through his eyes: strong and brave and selfless. She saw the pride in his face, and her heart felt like bursting. "So she went to the well?" she asked, breathless.

"It was not that simple," he said. His hand was damper now, more like flesh than wood. It was as if the memories were making him more alive. Maybe they are, she thought. "The only time she leaves the tower is after the witch banishes her to the desert. Shortly after, she finds me, wandering blind. Her tears touch my eyes, and then we begin again. It is impossible to change this pattern. Believe me, we tried, but our story would always find us."

"Then how . . . ?" she asked.

"It was Rapunzel's idea," he said, pride swelling his voice again. "She was the only one who truly understood how the Wild worked. It must complete its stories, you see. Rapunzel thought that the way for her to reach the well would be if I were there. We told no one—not the dwarves, not the witch—to limit the chance of the Wild interfering. Cinderella took me there in her pumpkin carriage without asking questions. She trusted Rapunzel that much. Once I was in place, the Wild saw to it that Rapunzel found me."

It was a smart plan, including relying on Cindy's trust.

Julie realized she'd never considered whether or not her mother was smart. She was just Mom. Mom the hairstylist. Mom the fairy tale. But now—Mom the hero. Never "just Mom" again. "And that worked?" Julie asked. "She made the wish?"

"No," he said. "It failed. Her tears fell before her wish could reach the well. We tried again and again. Even when I stood behind the well, even when I stood on top of the well, her tears touched me first. We tried again and again, I do not remember how many times. Perhaps hundreds. Perhaps thousands."

"But she made the wish," Julie insisted. "It worked, didn't it?"

He smiled then like the sun rising. "Yes, it must have worked. You are here. Five hundred years have passed." He looked around the throne room, wonder in his eyes. "Are we free of the Wild?"

Her throat clogged. How could she tell him? Unable to meet his eyes, she studied her feet, crusted in mud and flecks of blood. She glanced up. He must have seen the answer in her expression: his face crumpled. He took a breath as if to speak and then released it. He took another breath—gathering courage? "Rapunzel is not here," he said.

The way he said her mother's name made Julie's heart hurt. It made her think of shattered glass. "She's in a tower," Julie said. "She's in the Wild's tower. What is the last thing you remember?"

He was silent for a moment, studying her. "You will not like it," he said.

She heard a dull roaring in her ears. *You will not like it.* She knew what was coming: the reason why he had been left behind, the reason why she had grown up without a father. She nodded, understanding.

He continued to look at her as if reading something in her face—what did her face say? she wondered, what did he see when he looked at her? "What's your name?" he asked, suddenly changing the subject.

"Julie," she said, and realized in a rush she was relieved: she wasn't ready to hear whatever it was that she wasn't going to like. "Julie Marchen. *Märchen* means 'fairy tale' in German. I don't have a middle name. Mom didn't know kids had middle names." She stopped talking abruptly, realizing she was babbling. "What's your name?"

He was silent for a moment. "Rapunzel called me her prince."

"Nothing more specific?" Surely, Mom could have done better than that.

"You can name me, if you'd like," he said.

She didn't know what to say. How did you name your own father? "I want to call you 'Dad,'" she said.

"I would like that," he said.

Julie and her father lapsed into silence.

She took a deep breath. "I have to know," she said. "The last wish. I *need* to know."

He nodded. "It was a simple thing," he said. "A simple plan. We had tried most everything else." Julie didn't breathe. In his soft and calm voice, he said, "She came to the well, and I stood on the stones. As she reached me, she began to cry. And so I jumped into the well. Her tears fell, but I had fallen first."

"She made the wish before the tears could touch your eyes," Julie said.

"Yes," he said simply.

So that's what happened. The understanding felt like a wave, and Julie wanted to cry. Her father was a martyr, and her mother was a hero. In her mind's eye, she saw it: her father falling down the well, her mother leaning over . . . the tears fell, she made the wish . . . How had she made that wish? How had she let him fall?

"It was a simple plan," her father said. "Simple enough even for me. But so hard to do. We did not know what would happen to me when I fell into the well. We did not know if I would survive the fall. I did not know if she would forgive me if I didn't."

Not knowing whether he'd live or die, he had leapt, and she had wished. And the Wild had lost. "She's missed you," Julie said. As soon as she said it, she knew how true it was. "I've missed you."

For a moment, they were silent—a silence filled with

so many unspoken words that it felt loud. The castle soaked in the silence.

"You tell me now," he said. "Why have I missed five hundred years, and why am I awake now? How can the wish have worked and Rapunzel be in the tower? Why am I not riding through the woods? Why have I not forgotten?"

Julie took a deep breath. "Um, well, you see, apparently, someone made a new wish in Grandma's well while she was having dinner with us, and she went to stop it and then Mom went to save her. But I didn't know anything about it until I saw the Wild on TV . . ."

"What is TV?"

Despite everything, she burst out laughing. It was, she knew, tinged with hysteria. If she didn't laugh, she'd cry—and if she started crying, she wasn't sure she'd stop. Confused, her father half smiled. With an effort, she got herself under control, and she told her father her story.

When she finished, he studied her for a long while. She shifted from foot to foot. Was he going to say Cindy and Goldie shouldn't have let her into the Wild? Was he going to blame her for taking the lunch bag from Boots?

Instead, he said, "You were very brave."

Julie beamed. "You think so?"

"You're just like your mother," he said.

Julie thought she'd never heard a nicer compliment. She felt her eyes fill with tears. He laid his hand on her shoulder. She could smell him. She had never imagined his scent. He smelled a little like pine and a little like dust. He had been here a long time.

* * *

Julie spent the afternoon with him, telling him her stories and describing her life, trying to bridge the long years he'd missed. He was a good listener, laughing at her jokes and sympathizing at all the appropriate moments. In the evening, they ate dinner together, delicious dishes Julie didn't recognize that appeared on a table at the far end of the throne room. After dinner, Julie and her father explored the palace together, hand in hand.

In one room, there was an ornate carousel. Surprise made Julie laugh out loud. She didn't know what she had expected, but it wasn't anything so—the word that sprang to mind was *happy*. Unicorns and griffins rose up and down as the merry-go-round went round and round. She stepped inside the room. Overhead, the ceiling was painted blue with white fluffy clouds. The floor felt like real grass. Shyly, her father said, "Do you want to try it?"

Julie shook her head. "Let's see what else is here first."

Together, they opened other golden doors. One room held a ballroom with chandeliers and pillars of gold. Another held a banquet hall with suits of armor lining the walls. Another held a stable of horses. "I'll teach you to ride," her father said. It was her turn to smile shyly.

The next room held dozens of different instruments:

pianos, harps, violins. Another held every game imagina-ble: Monopoly, Risk, Scrabble, Pictionary, and a beautiful chess set of carved marble. "Ooh, let's play," Julie said. She set the pawns in a row.

"There are still more doors," her father said.

"All right," she said. As they explored, she began draw-ing up lists in her head of all the things she wanted to do with her father now that she had found him.

The kitchen was stocked with cakes and breads and ice creams. The nursery held the most incredible dollhouse Julie had ever seen. The gymnasium had basketball courts, a baseball diamond, and a swimming pool. The gardens had an ice rink. There was even an entertainment room with a TV. Julie turned it on and demonstrated it to her dad. She didn't recognize the channels, but it didn't mat-ter. Another room had an arcade. Another, a pool table. Another was a bowling alley. Another, a fabulous library with a shelf devoted entirely to her favorites. Everything Julie could have ever dreamed of was in this castle.

Except her mother. And her grandmother. And Gillian. And Boots.

Julie released her father's hand as if it had stung her. She had forgotten. Oh, God, she'd forgotten they were still in the Wild. She'd forgotten this wasn't real. She'd been caught up in just as much of a dream as after she'd eaten the apple, but she didn't have the excuse of no memory. How had she let that happen? How could she have forgotten?

Her father looked down at her. "What's wrong?"

She felt sick. This might have been the best afternoon of her life, but it wasn't hers. It was the Wild's. Suddenly, the stone walls felt darker, closer, and she thought of dungeon walls. This was just a pretty cage. All of this . . . "What story are we in?" she asked.

He seemed confused, but did she know that it wasn't an act? She blinked fast. Her eyes felt hot. Dad. Daddy. Did she know that the Wild wasn't controlling his every action? Did he know? "What do you mean?" he asked.

"You, me, the castle—what is it? Is there a spindle somewhere? A forbidden door? What?" Her voice cracked. Blinking faster, she took off walking down the hall. Don't cry, she told herself. Don't cry.

Her father followed. "Julie, I don't understand. Aren't you happy here?"

Yes, she was, and that's what made it all the worse. She wanted very badly to be wrong. She wanted to believe that this was real, that her father had spent these hours with her by choice, that he wasn't a puppet in the Wild's story . . . *Please, let me be wrong. Please* . . .

It didn't take her long to find what she was looking for. Julie wished that it had taken a lifetime. She walked up to it, the last door on the hallway—a wooden door with flaking purple paint, odd amid the golden doors. It had a modern doorknob and a peephole under a plastic sign. ROOM THIRTEEN, she read.

A motel room door.

"You may have all the wonders this castle has to offer," her father said in a wooden voice, "but you must not open this door."

Of course. She should have known. No matter how the Wild disguised this place with televisions and books and games, it had to make this castle from its old stories. It couldn't help itself. *The Wild has to play by its own rules,* her mom had said. *Remember that.* The Wild had to present her with this choice: either she could be the one who heeds the warning and stays or she could be the one who goes through the forbidden door and faces her fate. It was the only thing that made sense, the final game the Wild could play: she had to choose.

Her cheeks felt wet. She was crying, she realized. When had she started crying?

On the other side of this door was the Wishing Well Motel. On the other side of this door was the well, waiting for her to make the wish that would put everything back to normal.

Back to not fitting in. Back to Kristen laughing at her. Back to Mr. Wallace's history quizzes and Cindy's car rides and Mom's dinner parties . . .

Back to a world where everyone knew she was Rapunzel's daughter.

Their secret was out. Who knew what would happen? She could come home to find the media camped on her lawn. The tabloids would eat it up. The U.S. government could even be interested—the Wild had taken down a military helicopter, not to mention whatever else they'd thrown at it since. Scientists might probe and poke and study. She could be walking into a nightmare.

She could be walking into a world with no father.

Julie looked over her shoulder at her dad, and she felt her heart lurch into her throat. Dad. Her dad, alive and here. Candlelight behind him, he seemed to glow. *But I am offering a gift: the world as it should be*, the Wild had said. *In here, life is fair. Everyone has a place. Everyone belongs. I am offering you what you've always wanted.*

On the other side of this door was the real world, with all its embarrassments, disappointments, and losses. In here was happily ever after. Here was the father she'd always dreamed of having. Yes, he was the Wild's puppet, but he was here. She had a chance to make up for all those lost years. If she stayed with him, she would always belong. She would always have a role, the prince's daughter. The future wouldn't be a scary unknown. The Wild had made her a story of her own, cobbled together from the stories and people it knew she wanted, including a very special incentive: the one character who had not escaped its control. It was offering her a gift, and it was betting that she would take it. It was betting that she would choose to stay here and be forever safe. "Safe inside the Wild," she murmured.

And yet . . . five hundred years ago, Mom had chosen the real world over the Wild, and Dad had sacrificed himself to give it to her. Was this how Mom had felt when she looked down the well at her prince and had to make her wish? Julie felt as if she'd swallowed a tornado, and it was churning inside her, tearing her up.

In the Wild, Julie had gotten to be a hero. She'd flown on a griffin, outwitted an ogre, and danced at a ball. All in all, it was pretty wonderful.

Had Mom made the right choice? Was it worth it? Julie pictured her mother at home. She remembered how much they laughed together, like the time they'd thrown a surprise party for Gretel at the salon. She and Julie had made a cake, and the lit candles had come to life and cha-cha-ed out the door. They'd made it halfway down Main Street before Mom caught up to them with a fire extinguisher. Somehow, Julie didn't think moments like that happened in the Wild. Or little times, like movie nights, where Mom and Julie would rent movies, pop microwave popcorn, and make up their own ridiculous dialogue for the dramatic scenes. Or pizza nights, when they ate on the living room rug instead of the table and watched TV.

I envy them, the dwarf had said. *To have always been able to know who you are, to be able to change who you are, to make your own story . . .*

In that moment, Julie understood. It felt as if all the spinning pieces inside her had clicked into place, and she could see clearly now. Even if she was right about what would happen when the world knew about the Wild, it was worth it—it was worth the price. She went to her father and squeezed his hand. Her throat felt clogged, and she swallowed hard. "I understand why you weren't there while I was growing up," she told him. It was one of the hardest things she had ever had to say. She felt herself begin to cry again. So many years of blaming him . . . So many years of blaming her mother . . . Mom had to choose because she *had* to choose.

This castle, for everything it had, was not life. It wasn't real.

"Can you come with me?" she asked, already knowing the answer.

He shook his head. She had guessed right: the Wild owned him. He wasn't free. His presence here was part of another story, Julie's story.

She wished she had a camera. She'd replace those illustrations in her locker with photographs. He didn't look like any of them. She tried to memorize the crinkle of his eyebrows and the curves of his nose. She released his hand.

She expected him to ask or command her to stay, but he didn't. He touched her cheek, wet with tears, and said only one word: "Julie." It wasn't a question or a command. It was everything—it was everything all wrapped up in one word: her name. Julie Marchen, Rapunzel's daughter.

Turning away from her father, she twisted the doorknob.

It didn't open. She shook it. It was locked. "Dad?" she said, looking over her shoulder. Candles fizzled in their sconces, and the hall darkened. He was gone. "Dad!" She shook the doorknob again. Out of the darkness, she heard wind. It's coming. The Wild's coming.

She reached into her pocket for her wand, and she felt the key: Mom's special linen closet key. She pulled it out and shoved it into the lock. It melted in her hand to fit. She turned it and opened the door to the Wishing Well Motel.

Chapter Twenty-six
The Wishing Well Motel

Lifting up a veil of vines, Julie stooped under the leaves. She was at the front of the Wishing Well Motel beside the dry and cracked swimming pool. The Wild had not transformed anything here. It had merely grown over it, like the jungle over a lost Mayan temple, as if the growth had been hurried. The motel lay under a thick silence. The crunch of Julie's feet echoed.

It was eerie without the sound of TVs in the motel rooms or the Coke machine near the lobby. Grandma always had guests. Julie spotted half of the motel sign through the leaves. She went up to it and cleared the branches so that THE WISHING WELL MOTEL and the dull neon VACANCIES underneath it were visible. Grandma would have liked that. She lingered for an instant more, then realized she was delaying. After all she had gone through, now that she was here, she was afraid.

Of what? All she had to do now was find the well and make a wish. How hard could that be? She climbed through the tangle of plants that had once been the lawn. The well was behind the motel, and the fastest way there was through the lobby. She cleared vines from the door and opened it.

The lobby was dark. Covered in vines and leaves, the windows gave off only a dim, sickly green light. It reminded Julie of the magician's lair. Maybe she should go around. No, she could do this. Just cross through and out the opposite door. Julie stepped inside. She could do this, she repeated.

There were shapes hunched over the lobby's main desk. She crept across the room. Closer, she could see the shapes had fur. She knew them! They were the three bears, their heads down on the counter beside bowls of porridge. All three bears snored in unison. Drugged porridge, Julie guessed, or magicked. That explained how someone had been able to get past them to make a wish. Julie shivered. No wonder Goldie hadn't found them. The only bears who weren't dancing for Gillian were here, asleep since before the Wild was freed. I'll get us out of here, she promised silently. It's almost over.

In the dim green light, Julie skirted around them. As she passed Little Bear, he lifted his head. "Do you think it is that easy?" he said.

She froze. That tone of voice . . . she knew that flat, mechanical voice. Oh, no. "Little Bear?" She knew it wasn't.

"This one's too hot, this one's too cold, and now you will find the one that's just right?" the Wild said. "You won't find your happily ever after. Not this way."

It couldn't stop her now, could it? "I beat your games," Julie said. "I made it here. You have to let me go—your rules."

"You will make a foolish wish," the Wild said. "You will destroy your happiness and the happiness of your family and friends. No one has ever made the wish that was truly their heart's desire."

It was trying to talk her out of it. She *had* survived the stories. All the Wild had left was talk. Right? As if on cue, the other two bears raised their heads. "Someone has been eating my porridge. Someone has been sleeping in my bed."

Julie ran out the lobby door.

She skidded to a stop. Hip-high bushes and thick trees clogged the backyard. She shot a look over her shoulder. The bears weren't following her.

Maybe they couldn't—the bears never caught their Goldilocks.

Putting her hands on her knees, she caught her breath. It was just talk. Just talk. And it couldn't talk her out of this. She'd find the well, and she'd do what she had to do.

Julie peered into the vegetation. The well should be right in front of her. Just because she couldn't see it didn't mean it wasn't there. She climbed over vines and roots. She waded through bushes.

And she found the well. All of a sudden, it was there. There weren't any fanfares or lightning bolts or anything like that. She almost stumbled over it, in fact—the base of the well jutted out into her path and was hidden by bushes. Julie cleared aside the brambles and stepped onto the base. She wasn't sure what she was feeling. The well certainly didn't look like much.

Under a layer of moss, the wishing well looked as it always had: cracked mortar, dilapidated shingles, chipped stones. The rope that had once held a bucket was frayed. The bucket itself was centuries gone. Julie put both hands on the mossy wall and looked down. She couldn't see the bottom.

All right, then. Now what?

It was time to make a wish. Okay. She was ready. Julie rolled up her sleeves, spread her feet wide, braced herself on the wall, and leaned directly over the middle of the well.

What wish should she make?

She hadn't thought about it. Not specifically. She'd been so caught up in the race to get here that she hadn't thought about what she'd do when she got here.

She could wish it all had never happened. No, she

couldn't wish that. She thought of tricking the ogre into using the wand, dancing at the ball, meeting her father. She didn't want it to have never happened.

She could wish the Wild was gone. That idea was appealing. Not only could she stop the Wild here, but she could ensure that it never came back. She liked that. It would serve the Wild right for playing puppet master with who knew how many people.

But what would happen to all those people—not to mention herself—if the Wild disappeared while they were inside it? What if it took everyone with it? Julie shuddered. The Wild was right: she could make things worse if she wasn't careful. Far, far worse.

What had her mother wished for? Too bad Mom hadn't given her a hint. It has to be the wish dearest to your heart, her mother had said. But what was that wish? What did she want? She used to want so many things. Now she just wanted her life back.

That's my wish, she thought. I want my life back. But how should she say it so it didn't come out wrong? How could she guarantee that the wish she made was what she really wanted? *It has to be the wish that's dearest to your heart.*

Julie smiled. She knew what to say. Leaning over the mossy rocks, she whispered into the well, "I wish the wish that is dearest to my heart."

Her words fell like pennies into the water.

For an instant, there was silence. She looked around, peering at the still, dark forest that surrounded the motel like a waiting animal. It didn't work, she thought. After everything, it didn't work.

She turned in a slow circle, looking for some movement, for any movement. Should she make another wish? Was the well broken? Was it all a trick? What if she was trapped here forever? The trees were silent. Blinking, she wiped at her eyes. She was not going to cry. There had to be something else she could do. There had to be . . .

Her mother walked out of the woods.

She looked as if she'd been lost in the forest for days. Her face was tired, purple circles under her eyes and gray shadows on her cheeks. Her hair was shorn at odd angles, as if someone had cut it with a hedge trimmer. Her clothes were torn and stained with dirt. Julie thought she'd never looked more beautiful.

Zel halted. Her eyes widened. "Julie?"

Julie ran to her and threw her arms around her neck. "Oh, Julie," Zel said. She hugged her tight.

When Julie pulled back, both their cheeks were wet. Zel smiled through the tears. "You did it," Zel said. "You did it!"

Julie shook her head. "The Wild's still here. I didn't do it right."

"What did you wish?" her mother asked.

Julie told her.

"Oh, pumpkin," Zel said. She smiled as bright as the noon sun. Why is she smiling? Julie wondered—and then she realized why: Julie had wished for her heart's desire, and her mother had come. Mom was part of Julie's dearest wish. "Pumpkin, you did just right," Mom said. She hugged her again.

And there was a flash.

* * *

In an instant, Julie, Zel, and Gothel were sitting at the dinner table, leftover quiche on the plates in front of them. All three of them looked at each other. Outside, sirens started to wail. "Uh-oh," Zel said.

Gothel stood, knocking a plate of quiche onto the floor. "Rapunzel . . ."

Zel sprang out of her chair and rushed to the window.

"Is it the police?" Julie asked. She heard voices outside. Lots of voices. And helicopters. Julie joined her mother at the window. It was the police. And the military. And the media. News vans, cop cars, and army jeeps were zooming down West Street. She saw soldiers jump out of vehicles and knock on the neighbors' doors. It wouldn't be long until they came here too. "What do we do?" Julie asked.

"I will turn them into frogs," Gothel said. She withdrew a wand from the billows of her cape. "I will . . ." She swayed and then shook her head, as if trying to clear it.

Julie and Zel turned to her in alarm. Oh, no. Had she forgotten again? Was she the witch, not Grandma? Zel caught Gothel's arm, steadying her. "You will *not*," Zel said. "Mom, listen to me. We're free. You're free."

"I . . ." The witch stared at Rapunzel, and then Gothel's face crumbled. "I was the witch," she said softly. "Again. It was still my role. Oh, Zel, it knew—at my core, I am still the witch. I cannot be free of it."

Gently, Zel said, "Don't be ridiculous."

Julie backed away from the window as her grandmother—her strong, unflappable grandmother—began to cry. Julie had wanted to return to the real world. Her heart's desire had been to return to her real life. She had known there would be a price. This was the price: their secret was out. And she had lost her father. Again.

"Take a deep breath, Mother. We need to pull ourselves together and determine who made it out of the Wild," Zel said. "Did anyone other than the three of us make it?"

Julie hadn't thought of that. Had she wished for the wrong thing after all? Had the Wild found a way to make it come out wrong? Had she lost her father for nothing? No, she wouldn't believe it. Her heart's desire had to include everyone: Grandma. Boots. Cindy, Goldie, the bears . . . Gillian! What happened after the ball? Had she gotten free of the animals? Had she gotten free of the Wild? Julie had to try to call her. She bolted upstairs.

She flung open her bedroom door and halted in the doorway. On her bed slept an orange cat in doll-sized pj's. Beside him, in a baby's nightgown, was a white, longhaired cat. "Boots?" Julie said.

He opened one eye. "Hey, sis," Boots said.

Suddenly, she felt as if she were brimming inside. Her vision blurred—there were tears in her eyes. He was okay! He'd made it out! She'd done it right!

Boots said, "Meet my girlfriend." He nudged the white cat.

The white cat blinked awake and said, "Oh, yes, nice to meet you. Sorry I was evil before. I'm feeling much better now."

Julie yanked up the dust ruffle and saw it, the Wild, as a small tangle of green. It was back. The Wild was home too. Outside, a siren wailed, loud and close, and a green, leafy vine withdrew deeper under the bed.

She started to laugh and cry at the same time. *This*— all of it, all of them—was her dearest wish! Still laughing and crying, she scooped both cats into her arms and hugged them.

"Watch the fur!" they said in unison.

Releasing them, Julie picked up the phone and dialed. Her hands were shaking. Please, she thought, please let everything be back to normal. Gillian answered, "Yes-th?" Gillian! Oh, was she glad to hear that voice! And the trumpet—she couldn't wait to hear that trumpet! "You okay?" Julie asked.

"My wips are sore."

"What?"

"My *lips* are sore."

She winced. Gillian must have played for hours. It must have been torture. "Sorry!"

"S'okay," Gillian said. "Some parts were terrible, yeah. But Mom says-th I can keep a dancing bear. S'that's kinda cool. What 'appened to you?"

"Well . . ." Some parts *were* terrible, but others . . . She grinned. Yeah, it was kind of cool. Phone to her ear, Julie flopped backward onto the bed. "First, my bike came alive . . ."

Chapter Twenty-seven
Happily Ever After

Three weeks later . . .

Julie dove at her backpack. "Oh, no, you don't!" She grabbed the straps as the Wild attempted to pull her backpack under the bed. "Let go!" She kicked at a vine. "I'll prune you!" She gave it another solid kick.

The vines released, and she fell backward onto her butt. Ow. That was totally unnecessary. She glared at the Wild, then she got to her feet and examined the backpack. Part of the transformation had already begun: half of the backpack looked like a vagabond's pack. The nylon was now patched rags. Great. Just great. She opened it. Luckily, her books were fine. The Wild hadn't had it long enough to affect them.

"Julie!" her mom called from downstairs. "Cindy's here!"

"Coming!" she yelled back. Julie gave the Wild another glare. "Behave yourself," she said. She left the room and locked it behind her.

She passed through the kitchen. On the kitchen table, Grandma had spread a map of Europe. "Don't nag me, Zel," she was saying. "I don't need reservations. Plenty of our kind still live there."

"You can cancel the reservations if everything works out," Zel said. Julie could hear the irritation in her mother's voice. They'd been arguing about this for two days now, ever since Grandma had announced her plans and handed her motel over to the three bears. Julie fetched her lunch, leftover ravioli from the latest dwarf dinner, from the refrigerator.

"I will be there to make amends," Gothel said. "They won't refuse to offer hospitality once they understand I mean them no harm."

"It's been centuries. You can't just drop in unannounced." Pausing mid-argument, she gave Julie a kiss. "Have an uneventful day, pumpkin." With a backward wave, Julie went out the door.

Outside, Cindy was waiting in her orange Subaru. Julie climbed in, and Cindy sparkled at her with a thousand-watt smile. "You won't believe the night I had," Cindy gushed as she threw the car into reverse and peeled out of the driveway.

Julie clutched her seat belt. Maybe Mom would let her take the bus again soon. Really, it was much better than it had been the first week. There were far fewer reporters pestering people on the street or kids at bus stops. She shouldn't be so overprotective. Despite all the FBI and reporters and scientists that had appeared that first week, no one knew how intimately Julie and her family were involved in the whole Wild phenomenon. Only Julie and her mother had been at the well, and they weren't telling.

Cindy squealed the brakes in front of the school. As Julie got out, Cindy gave a cheery wave and a shout reminding Julie to watch who she kissed. Julie winced.

Next week, she was definitely taking the bus. She trudged into school and down the hall toward her locker. "Oh, how vintage," a familiar voice said from across the hall.

Kristen was smirking at Julie's backpack. Her bevy of friends giggled. Julie walked past her without a word. Gillian was waiting beside Julie's locker. "If she only knew what you did," Gillian whispered. "You saved her."

Even Gillian didn't know all that Julie had done. She didn't know about the door in the castle. She didn't know Julie had given up her father. Julie pushed down the familiar ache. She'd made her choice. She'd known the price. "It's okay," she said.

"It's not okay," Gillian said. "I don't know how you can stand it."

Julie glanced back across the hall. Honestly? She didn't care what Kristen thought or said. Not anymore. Or at least not much. Kristen was Kristen. Just like Julie was Julie. Her father wasn't the only one she'd gotten to know in the Wild. She changed the subject: "Ready for band tryouts?"

Gillian grinned. "You bet. No one can say I haven't been practicing." Her dancing bear insisted on it. Julie thought she'd make first trumpet for sure.

"Luck," Julie said. She held out her pinky, and Gillian shook it with her pinky.

"Luck to you on the Wallace quiz," Gillian said.

"Piece of cake," Julie said. "Boots's girlfriend and I have been studying."

Gillian picked up her trumpet case as Julie switched her homework books with her books for first period. Gently, Julie pressed the palm of her hand against the illustrations of Rapunzel's prince on the inside of her locker door. "Wish me luck, Dad," she whispered.

And she and Gillian went to class.

Epilogue

Across town, in the children's section of the Northboro Public Library, Linda the librarian hummed to herself as she shelved brand-new volumes of fairy tales: *The Swan Soldiers, Puss-in-Boots and the Wild Bicycles, The Girl and the Griffin, Goldilocks and the Beanstalk, The Mysterious Princess from Unknown Lands, The Wishing Well Motel* . . . All total, she had twenty-four new books.

Exactly what she'd wished for.

In the darkness, the heart of the fairy tale waited . . .